PUFFI

Sky Horses
The Eye of the Storm

The fourth book in the quartet

Linda Chapman lives in Leicestershire with her family and two Bernese mountain dogs. When she is not writing, she spends her time looking after her two young daughters and baby son, horse riding and talking to people about writing.

You can find out more about Linda on her websites t *lindachapman.co.uk* and *lindachapmanauthor.co.uk*

Books by Linda Chapman

BRIGHT LIGHTS

CENTRE STAGE

MY SECRET UNICORN series

NOT QUITE A MERMAID series

SKY HORSES series

STARDUST series

UNICORN SCHOOL series

LINDA CHAPMAN

Sky Horses

The Eye of the Storm

Illustrated by Ann Kronheimer

PUFFIN

PUFFIN BOOKS

Published by the Penguin Group
Penguin Books Ltd, 80 Strand, London WC2R ORL, England
Penguin Group (USA) Inc., 375 Hudson Street, New York, New York 10014, USA
Penguin Group (Canada), 90 Eglinton Avenue East, Suite 700, Toronto, Ontario, Canada M4P 2Y3
(a division of Pearson Penguin Canada Inc.)
Penguin Ireland, 25 St Stephen's Green, Dublin 2, Ireland (a division of Penguin Books Ltd)
Penguin Group (Australia), 250 Camberwell Road, Camberwell, Victoria 3124, Australia
(a division of Pearson Australia Group Pty Ltd)
Penguin Books India Pvt Ltd, 11 Community Centre, Panchsheel Park, New Delhi – 110 017, India
Penguin Group (NZ), 67 Apollo Drive, Rosedale, North Shore 0632, New Zealand
(a division of Pearson New Zealand Ltd)
Penguin Books (South Africa) (Pty) Ltd, 24 Sturdee Avenue, Rosebank,
Johannesburg 2196, South Africa

Penguin Books Ltd, Registered Offices: 80 Strand, London WC2R ORL, England

puffinbooks.com

First published 2009
1

Text copyright © Linda Chapman, 2009
Illustrations copyright © Ann Kronheimer, 2009
All rights reserved

The moral right of the author and illustrator has been asserted

Set in Bembo 15/22pt
Typeset by Palimpsest Book Production Limited, Grangemouth, Stirlingshire
Made and printed in England by Clays Ltd, St Ives plc

British Library Cataloguing in Publication Data
A CIP catalogue record for this book is available from the British Library

ISBN: 978-0-141-32333-6

www.greenpenguin.co.uk

Penguin Books is committed to a sustainable future
for our business, our readers and our planet.
The book in your hands is made from paper
certified by the Forest Stewardship Council.

To Iola, who always reads my books first
and whose comments are so important.
Sky Horses was written for you.

When the dark one returns, the door shall be reopened
And danger will threaten all living below.
If the binding is broken, they can be protected,
But one coming willingly lets the dark's power grow
Until the first gateway is split by magic
And he who is trapped is free to go.

Two gateways now balance the light and the darkness,
One lost in memory, hidden by the sea.
The dark door is reserved for the hand that creates it.
The other lies close to a whispering tree,
Deep underground and made from moonlight.
When it is found, then two can be free.

Yet danger is found with the new gateway —
Beware the dark horse who leaps for the sky.
With arrow of fire and grey feather's direction,
Two must help here or all hopes will die.
If the darkest impostor is not defeated,
Then never again will the cloud stallion fly.

One

Erin sat on the window seat in her bedroom, writing in a diary. A second diary, an old leather-bound one, lay beside her. Pushing her long dark-blonde hair back behind her ears, she read over what she had just written.

Dear Mum,
I've decided to write to you because so much is happening and though you aren't here any more I know you would understand. I love Jo

and I'm glad she and Dad are married now, but of course I can't tell them anything about stardust or weather weaving and it's all getting so scary. I've been reading your diary — the two-year one you had when you were ten and eleven. I'm glad you wrote down so much about magic.

Erin picked up a stone from her window ledge. It had a hole in the centre. She held it up and looked through the hole at the clouds in the evening sky. Now she could see they weren't just clouds, but a landscape with distinct hills and valleys, rivers and meadows. Beautiful horses of all different shades of grey moved slowly through their cloud world, their manes and tails sweeping to the floor.

Sky horses.

Erin bit her lip. She knew now that sky horses controlled the weather. When they were quiet, the skies were calm; when they moved about, clouds formed and rain fell. Erin remembered the first time she had seen them, almost a month ago. Back then, she had thought she was completely ordinary, just eleven-year-old Erin Davies who loved horses and lived with her dad, three stepbrothers and stepmum, Jo. But in one day she had found out that magic was real, sky horses existed and that she was a rare kind of stardust spirit, a weather weaver, who could work magic using special stones called hagstones.

Erin put the stone down and glanced at the diary beside her. Her mum had been a weather weaver too. *Oh, Mum,* she thought longingly. *I really wish you were here.*

She picked up her pen again and carried on writing:

If you were here, you would help show me the weather-weaving magic I need to do to stop Marianne. She's gone into the clouds, Mum. It's horrible.

A memory flashed vividly into Erin's mind. Her pen hesitated over the paper as, for a moment, she saw Marianne, a dark stardust spirit, standing on top of a cliff, holding out a hagstone. A black mist was pouring out through the hole in the centre of the stone. It formed a swirling circle – a magic gateway into the sky horses' world. Marianne had transformed into a horse and she had jumped through the gateway. Now she was up there. But she shouldn't be. It was all wrong. Erin quickly started writing again.

You said in your diary that humans shouldn't go into the cloud world – that it makes the horses sick and makes their magic flow away. Well, Marianne's gone up there because she wants to control them. She doesn't care that they will get ill. She just wants to have complete power over the weather so that everyone is scared of her. Tor says she could start a huge storm just like there was years and years ago before even Granny was born. People and animals could be injured and killed. There would be loads of damage. We have to stop her and find a way for Tor and Mistral to get back to their kingdom.

Despite her anxiety, Erin couldn't help but smile as she thought of Tor, the majestic sky stallion, and his son, a young mischievous colt called Mistral. They were

trapped on Earth at the moment, living in the woods near Erin's house, but both of them longed to get back to the sky.

Oh, Mum, I wish you could meet Tor — and Mistral. They're amazing. Marianne captured Tor and then trapped Mistral too; that's why they're here. They're free from her now. Me and Chloe — she's my best friend and a stardust spirit too — are going to try to help them get back to the clouds using the magic gateway that's hidden in the cliffs, the one you wrote about in your diary. The trouble is, of course, that it can only be used when the tide is out, otherwise you just can't reach it. But when Tor does get to use it and returns to the sky, he's going to fight Marianne and chase her back to Earth, and when she gets here we have to destroy the dark gateway she has made using a hagstone so she

*can't go into the cloud world again. But I'm
scared, Mum. I have to destroy the gateway all
by myself. Although Tor can help me by telling
me what to do, he can't do the magic and Chloe
isn't a weather weaver — she can only do
normal stardust magic. So, it's all down to me.
But what if I can't do it? Marianne is so
powerful. How can I possibly fight her? I really
wish you were here . . .*

'Erin!'

Erin broke off as she heard her dad
calling her from the landing.

'Time to get ready for bed!' he called.

Erin quickly shut the diary. 'OK!'

*I don't know how we'll do it, but we'll stop
Marianne,* she thought. *We'll get her out of
Tor and Mistral's kingdom.*

She looked out of the window. There

were bands of clouds across the pale early-evening sky now. Swirling shafts of golden sun shot through the clouds like thin columns of light. It was a beautiful sight. But Erin felt as if an icy hand was running along her spine. It was as if she was seeing the magic flowing away from the sky horses down to the ground. She thought of the horses up there who would grow weaker and weaker, thought of the massive storms that might come, and bit her lip. She and Chloe would stop Marianne — they had to before it was too late.

Two

Erin changed into her pyjamas. She could hear her stepbrothers arguing about what TV channel to watch in the lounge.

Jo, her stepmum, was in the kitchen, unloading the dishwasher. She smiled as Erin came in. 'Hi, Erin. Would you like a hot chocolate?'

'I'll get it,' said Erin, seeing how tired Jo looked. 'Shall I make you a cup of tea at the same time?'

Jo smiled. 'Yes, please. I've been running

around all day trying to get things packed up for the boys.'

Sam and Ben, Erin's two eldest stepbrothers, were going to Wales for a sailing weekend the next morning and Jake, her twelve-year-old stepbrother, had a tennis tournament in Birmingham.

'So, how are you?' Jo asked as Erin got two mugs out. 'I've been so busy recently with all the boys' sporting activities and you've been at the stables day and night it seems – I feel like I haven't seen you at all. What have you been up to?'

Erin wondered what Jo would say if she replied, *Oh, you know, flying around at night, trying to find a hidden gateway that leads to the clouds, fighting a dark spirit . . .*

'Nothing much,' she said, shrugging. 'Just going to the stables and stuff.' Erin rode at Hawthorn Stables. She had lessons there and helped with the ponies. Now she was eleven and the nights were lighter, her dad and Jo had started letting her cycle there after school too.

'How's Kestrel?' asked Jo.

'He's great!' Erin enthused. Kestrel was a grey, part-Arab pony. He was new to the riding school and Jackie, the owner of the stables, had asked her if she would help look after him because he was having trouble settling in.

Jo looked at her. 'I was talking to Jackie the other day and she was saying that she's not sure he's cut out to be a riding-school pony, but she seems very pleased with how you're getting on with him.'

Erin frowned. 'He's fine whenever I ride him. I'm sure he'll soon get used to being ridden by lots of people. He just needs a bit more time. What else did Jackie say? Why were you talking to her?'

'No real reason,' Jo said, shrugging. She changed the subject. 'So, how's Chloe getting on with Ziggy? Her mum was saying she's over the moon about him.'

Ziggy was Chloe's new pony. She had got him for her birthday three days ago.

'Yeah.' Erin tried not to sigh. She'd always longed for a pony herself, but she knew her dad and Jo couldn't afford to buy one. She'd been trying very hard not to be jealous of Chloe having Ziggy. At least she had Kestrel, and Chloe kept saying that she could ride Ziggy as much as she liked.

'It must be hard not to mind,' said Jo, as if reading her thoughts.

'It is a bit,' Erin confided, handing her a mug of tea. 'But I'm glad Chloe's happy.'

Jo smiled at her. 'That's because you're a real friend. I'm proud of you.' She gave her a quick hug. 'Now, bedtime.'

'Can I read for half an hour?'

Jo nodded. 'And then light off.'

Erin went upstairs. In just a few hours she would be able to turn into her stardust self and go to meet up with

Chloe, Tor and Mistral. She took a deep
breath. What was the night going to hold?

'I believe in stardust. I believe in stardust.
I believe in stardust!'

As Erin whispered the final word, she
shot up into the air, her pyjamas becoming
a glittering pale-blue dress as she turned
into a stardust spirit. There were four types
of stardust spirit – spring, summer, autumn
and winter – and they each wore different-
coloured clothes: spring spirits wore green,
summer spirits wore gold, autumn spirits
wore silver and winter spirits wore blue.
They could also each do different magic.
Erin was a winter spirit who could make
it rain, hail or snow. Chloe was a summer
spirit, which meant she could heat things
up and start fires. Some stardust spirits had

extra-special powers like weather weaving. Erin was only just learning what she could do. She could use hagstones – stones with holes in the centre – to make magic things happen. So far Tor had shown her how to use the stones to see visions, to talk to him and to protect herself. Sometimes the stones showed her visions of things she hadn't asked to see. Tor said she must trust the magic in the stones; sometimes they would help her even when she didn't ask. It was cool she had learnt so much, but she knew there was still so much else she had to learn.

Now Erin flew out of the window and into the dark night. '*Camouflagus*,' she whispered. All stardust spirits could camouflage themselves, disappearing into the background so they appeared invisible. Erin headed towards the cliff tops, away from the village of Long Medlow where she lived. Heavy clouds were scudding across the night sky and the salt-filled wind buffeted her body.

Chloe was waiting for her on the shingle beach where they nearly always met, the waves lapping near her feet. 'Hi!' she called as Erin let her camouflage fade.

She flew up to meet Erin, her dark-brown curls bouncing on her shoulders, her gold dress swirling. 'Isn't it windy tonight? I heard on the TV there's a big storm coming.'

Erin nodded. 'I hope it's not really bad.'

Chloe looked worried. 'I bet it's Marianne, up in the sky causing trouble. I wish we could get to the hidden gateway in the cliffs so that Tor and

Mistral could go back to the sky and stop her. But with the tide coming in like this there's no way we can get to it.'

'Tor and I might be able to stop the storm, even from down here,' said Erin, knowing she could use her weather-weaving powers.

'I wish I was a weather weaver and could do something,' sighed Chloe. 'You're really lucky!'

Erin didn't feel lucky sometimes, but she knew Chloe wouldn't believe her. 'Come on. Let's go and find him.'

As Erin and Chloe swooped down into the clearing in the centre of the woods, two grey horses emerged from the trees – a beautiful white stallion with wise dark eyes and a smaller, dark-grey colt with a sticking-up mane and a cheeky expression. The colt whinnied a shrill greeting.

Chloe flew down and hugged him. 'Hello, Mistral.' The colt butted her with his head, making her almost fall over.

Meanwhile Erin landed beside Tor.

The sky stallion whickered softly. 'The horses are in turmoil in the skies, Erin,' he said. 'We must use your magic tonight to try to calm them.'

Erin could use her weather-weaving powers to send a vision of Tor into the sky. While his body stayed on Earth, an image of him appeared in the clouds so he could move among the other sky horses and talk to them, calm them and lead them. She had worked this kind of magic lots of times before, but not since

Marianne had gone through the gateway
the other night.

'What about Marianne?' she asked.
'She'll be there.'

'Yes, Father,' said Mistral, looking
round anxiously. 'What if the dark spirit
sees your image? Won't she try to hurt
you or fight you?'

'Will she be able to if you're just an
image?' asked Chloe.

'She will,' replied Tor. 'But it's a risk I
will have to take.'

Erin and Chloe marked out a large circle with stones on the forest floor. Tor stepped inside it and then Erin knelt down and took a hagstone out of her pocket. She looked at the hole in the centre of it and let her mind go blank. The shadow in the hole seemed to swell.

'Sky horses, come,' she whispered, feeling her fingers tingling with magic.

Tor's body dissolved into a cloud of mist. He shrank down until he was the size of a small model horse. Around the edges of the circle sky horses began to appear, young and old. They moved about quickly, some trotting, others cantering, other rearing up. Erin knew she was seeing a picture of what was happening up in the clouds.

Snowdance, Tor's lead mare and

Mistral's mother, came trotting over to him. She was a beautiful grey mare with large eyes. They nuzzled each other in greeting and then Tor swiftly began to move among the herd, calming them. Suddenly though, to Erin's surprise, the horses in the circle began to dissolve into mist and fade away.

Erin blinked. What was happening? The sky horses had all vanished. There was just Tor left.

'Sky horses, come,' she said quickly. A few wisps of mist swirled across the circle, but then they too disappeared.

'What's happening?' Chloe demanded from outside the circle.

'Why have you stopped using your magic, Erin?' whinnied Mistral.

'I–I haven't,' Erin stammered in

surprise. 'One minute I was doing it. The next the horses just disappeared.' Her eyes flew to Tor's. He was now growing back to full size again. 'Was it Marianne, Tor? Was she doing something to stop me – to stop us from calming the horses?'

Tor sighed heavily. 'Not directly. It is *your* magic, Erin.' He shook his head. 'I was worried this would be the case. Your magic powers are being weakened by the dark gateway Marianne has made.'

'What do you mean?' asked Erin.

'It is because Marianne used one of your hairs to create that gateway,' said Tor. 'Hair holds power and if one weather weaver has the hair of another they can draw on that other weather weaver's power. As you know, when Marianne made the gateway she used one of your hairs and one of your mother's from your mother's old diary. The dark gateway is now drawing on your power, weakening your magic, and it will continue to do so for as long as it exists.'

'So my weather-weaving powers will get weaker and weaker?' asked Erin slowly.

Tor nodded.

'What can we do about it, Father?' demanded Mistral.

'The only way to stop it happening is to destroy the dark gateway,' Tor answered. 'But that will take a lot of power.'

Chloe frowned. 'But you're saying that Erin doesn't have much power at the moment, so how is she going to do it?'

Tor hesitated. 'I do not know,' he admitted at last.

Alarm shot through Erin. She tried to get it clear in her head. 'So, even if we can get Marianne back here and get the hagstone that she made the gateway with so that we can destroy it, I still might not be able to do the magic?' She pushed her hands through her hair. 'This is pointless then!'

'It's not pointless!' Chloe said quickly. 'We'll be able to do this. Remember, Xanthe and Allegra are coming tomorrow. I bet Xanthe will be able to give you some advice.'

Xanthe was Chloe's godmother and Allegra was her daughter. They were both stardust spirits. Xanthe was a very powerful one and she had helped Erin and Chloe before.

Looking into Chloe's hazel eyes, Erin

felt her doubts fade. Chloe was right. They would be able to do it somehow. She nodded.

Chloe turned to Tor. 'I know! Couldn't Erin use her mum's hair to make herself more powerful? You told us a while ago that blood links are really important in weather weaving, that if you use the hair of one of your relatives in a spell their power adds to yours. Maybe there's still one of Erin's mum's hairs somewhere in the old diary. One that Marianne didn't find.'

'Even if there is a hair still in the diary, it would not help,' said Tor. 'Because Marianne is using both Erin's and her mother's hairs to create the dark gateway, all that power is being used up. The only way Erin could get more power is to use the hair of another weather weaver, and it would need to be someone related to Erin.'

'I don't have any other relatives who are weather weavers,' Erin said. 'Well, apart from Marianne.' A shiver ran through her. She had recently found out that Marianne was over a hundred years old. She didn't look like it because she used her magic to stay young and beautiful – but she was Erin's great-grandmother's sister. She had once before tried to take control of the skies by capturing a cloud stallion and Erin now knew that her great-grandmother had stopped her. That was when there had been the first big storm. *Will I be able to stop her this time?* Erin thought.

Chloe seemed to read her mind.

'There's no way we're going to let Marianne win,' she declared determinedly. 'We'll think of something.'

Tor stamped a hoof. 'You are right, Chloe. We *will* find a way.' As he spoke, the wind seemed to blow even more strongly. Around the clearing the trees creaked as their branches swayed in the wind. There was a loud crack and they all jumped back just in time as a heavy bough broke off a tree and crashed to the ground in front of them.

'You should get home,' Tor said quickly. 'The storm is still a little way off, but when it breaks you do not want to be outside.'

'We'll see you tomorrow,' said Erin, feeling very worried.

'Xanthe and Allegra will be with us,' added Chloe.

In the far distance there was a faint rumble of thunder. 'Go!' urged Tor.

The two girls rose quickly into the air.

'See you tomorrow!' Erin cried as she and Chloe flew away.

As they made their way back to the village, Erin thought over what had happened. It was horrible to think that the dark gateway was using up her power. *But I can still do some things*, she realized. *I used a hagstone to see the sky horses earlier*

this evening. She felt puzzled. Surely if her powers were weak she shouldn't have been able to do that?

When she got home, she quickly turned back from being a stardust spirit and then sat down on her bed with one of Tor's hairs that she always kept wound round her watchstrap. It let her speak to him whenever she wanted to, even if she didn't have a hagstone with her.

She held it in her cupped hands. 'Tor,' she said softly. 'Tor, are you there?'

'I am.' Tor's warm voice came into her mind.

'Tor, I can see the horses in the sky still. My powers must be OK,' she pointed out.

'No, Erin, they're not,' responded Tor gently. 'You do not need much power yourself to see the horses in the sky. You just need to free the stone's magic. It is very different when you are sending visions or creating them, as you do when you send an image of me into the clouds. That requires deep power from you.'

'Oh.' Erin's heart sank. 'At least we can still talk using this hair from your mane.'

She could almost hear the smile in Tor's warm voice. 'Yes. At least we can still do that.'

Erin squeezed the hair tight. If she shut her eyes, she could almost imagine him next to her.

'I'll see you tomorrow,' she told him softly.

'Yes. Sleep well,' said Tor.

Erin carefully wound the hair back round her watchstrap. Picking up her diary, she started writing to her mum, telling her everything that had happened that night. She wrote three whole pages.

It's so scary to think that my power's being weakened, she finally finished. *I don't know what we're going to do. I'm glad I can still talk to Tor though.* She hesitated as a thought crossed her mind. *It's going to be weird if he ever does get back to his kingdom*, she wrote. *We won't be able to see him and Mistral then. Well, not much anyway. Hopefully they'll still be able to come through the gateway and visit us sometimes. But it won't be the same.*

Erin stopped writing. She didn't want to think about that and, anyway, first they had to get Marianne out of the skies and defeat her. She closed her diary and then, turning off the light, she curled up under the duvet and fell into a fitful sleep.

CHAPTER
Three

When Erin woke up the next day, the wind was blustering outside and drops of rain were spattering on the window. She went downstairs. Her dad, Jake, Sam and Ben were in the kitchen having breakfast.

'Morning, sweetheart,' her dad said, as she sat down. 'Do you want some toast?'

'Yes, please,' she answered, picking up the cereal packet and starting to read the back of it. Jake swiped it. 'I was reading that!' Erin protested.

'Weirdo!' Jake grinned. 'You get more loopy every day.'

'You can talk!' retorted Erin as Jake poured a bowl of cereal and put orange juice on top. 'I mean, who has orange on –'

'Quiet, everyone! The weather forecast's coming on!' Sam interrupted. 'I want to hear what the weather's going to be like in Pembrokeshire.'

The presenter's voice rang out of the radio. '*Storms are approaching the south coast of England and residents are being warned to prepare for flooding. Gale-force winds and heavy rain are expected. Further north the weather should be calmer with overcast skies and mild winds.'*

'I'm glad our sailing course isn't here,' said Ben. 'Hopefully we should be OK in Wales.'

Erin's dad looked at Erin in concern. 'Maybe you shouldn't go to the stables today. It sounds like the weather is going to get even worse and it's not as if you'll be able to ride in this wind anyway.'

'There's still the mucking out and grooming to do,' said Erin. 'And we can clean tack if we can't ride.'

'It's great you're so dedicated, but I'm not sure you should be out all day. I might give Nicky a ring and see what she thinks.'

Chloe's mum, Nicky, had invited Erin over for tea that day. Erin and Chloe had been delighted because it meant Erin would be there when Allegra and Xanthe arrived. Erin's dad picked up the phone and dialled Chloe's number. Erin listened in. From her dad's side of the conversation it sounded as if Chloe was insisting on going to the stables too.

'Yes, Erin's saying she still wants to go,' Erin heard her dad saying to Nicky. 'I'm not sure with the bad weather that's been predicted . . . yes, I know . . . yeah, it is good they want to . . .' There was a pause. 'No. No decisions on that front yet. Jo and I are still thinking about it. Well, if you think it's OK, then I'll drop Erin off there with a packed lunch as usual. Thanks, Nicky. Bye.'

He put the phone down.

Erin vaguely wondered what Jo and
her dad were thinking about, but there
was a more important question to be
answered. 'So I can still go today?'

Her dad nodded. 'Nicky will come and
take you back to her house if the weather
starts to get worse.'

Erin breathed out in relief. She
couldn't wait to see Kestrel.

'I can't believe you want to go to the
stables in this weather,' Ben said to her.
'Just to see dumb horses and brush them.'

'Told you she was mad,' said Jake
cheerfully.

Erin glared at her stepbrothers.
Sometimes she really wished she was an
only child like Chloe!

★

37

After breakfast, Erin got dressed. She picked up the hagstone from her window ledge and looked at the sky. The horses seemed restless and unhappy; some were trotting with their ears back, others were standing with their heads down, their eyes dull. *They look like they're sick*, Erin thought. She knew it must be their magic seeping away.

She moved the stone across the sky and saw a horse with a coal-black coat charging at a group of mares with young foals. It was Marianne as a sky horse!

The mares and foals scattered in fear. Marianne reared up, striking out at them with her front legs.

'Erin! Are you almost ready?' her dad called.

Erin swung round. 'Just a minute!' She

looked back at the sky. The other horses had fled, leaving Marianne alone. As Erin watched, the dark spirit's horse-shaped body shivered and dissolved, narrowing and straightening as she transformed into her human shape. She was wearing a pale-blue dress and her long blonde hair blew around her. She turned and looked straight at Erin.

'*I can feel you watching me, Erin.*'

Erin jumped about a foot in the air. She tried to look away, but she found she couldn't. Her eyes wouldn't obey her.

'*I can sense you,*' Marianne's voice hissed into her head. '*I know you want to stop me, but you never will. I will make the sky horses do whatever I want. The weather is mine to control now. No weather weaver will ever be more powerful than me.*'

Erin's heart was pounding, but she

forced the words out. 'W–we'll stop you,' she stammered out loud.

'*You!*' Marianne laughed. '*If you try . . .*' she paused for a moment, '*you – and all those around you – will be very, very sorry.*'

Throwing back her head, she changed back into a black horse again and reared up triumphantly.

'Erin?'

There was a knock at Erin's door. Her dad looked in. 'Who are you talking to?' The shock broke the spell. Erin dropped the stone.

'Whoa!' said her dad as the stone bounced across the room and banged into the wardrobe door. 'Careful, Erin! Whatever are you doing?'

'N–nothing,' Erin stammered, hurrying to pick up the hagstone, her cheeks blazing.

'Come on then,' her dad said. 'We'd better go.'

Slipping the stone into her pocket, Erin nodded and hurried shakily after him.

All the way to the stables, Erin tried to put the conversation with Marianne out of her mind, but the words echoed round her head: *if you try, you – and all those around you – will be very, very sorry . . .*

As they pulled into the car park, Erin saw Chloe being dropped off. She ran over

to meet her. 'I've got something to tell you.'
She quickly told Chloe about the vision.

'That's horrid!' Despite her worry,
though, Chloe smiled. 'Bet your dad must
have thought you'd gone mad. Talking to
yourself and throwing stones!'

'I know,' groaned Erin. 'He already
thinks I'm strange because I don't want to
spend every minute of the day playing
sport like he used to.' She sighed. 'He's
always telling me I should be outside more,
getting fresh air, not sitting in my room.'

As they walked on to the yard, it
started to rain. Jackie was in her office.
'You're my only two helpers today.
Everyone else has rung to say they won't
be here. Thanks for coming. I really
appreciate it. Could you start by filling
some haynets please?'

Erin and Chloe nodded and headed up to the barn, bending their heads to avoid the rain.

'At least Fran and Katie aren't here today,' said Erin, as they started to fill haynets, shaking up the slices of hay until it was loose and then stuffing it into the empty nets.

Fran and Katie were two of the other helpers. They went to the same school as Erin and she had once been friends with them, but ever since they had discovered she would be going to a different secondary school in September, they had started being really mean to her. Fran was the worst. Chloe was always telling Erin she should stand up to them, but Erin hated arguments. She felt really glad she didn't have to see them that day.

They filled all the haynets and carried them two at a time to the stables. It was hard with the wind blowing into them.

'Can you help me shut the top stable doors, girls?' Jackie called, coming out of one of the stables. 'Then I think it might be best if we get all the ponies in from the field. I don't like the look of the sky.'

Erin and Chloe helped close the top doors of the stables, their fingers slipping on the cold wet metal, and then they set off for the fields. In the first field, four of the ponies – Ziggy, Pippin, Smoky and Tango – were sheltering by the gate, while the remaining four ponies in the field were trotting around anxiously, heads up, ears flickering.

The girls worked quickly, clipping lead ropes on and stroking and reassuring the

ponies before leading them up to the barn.
Back and forth they went, catching ponies
and bringing them in. It started to rain
more heavily. Their coats kept their bodies
dry, but the rain streamed over their faces
and bare hands and soaked through their
jodhpurs. The sky turned darker, becoming
the colour of a black bruise. There was a
loud rumble of thunder.

'Just Magpie and Kestrel to get in
now,' Chloe said to Erin.

'Hurry up, girls!' Jackie called. She was
leading two horses in. 'Once Kestrel and
Magpie are in the barn I think we should

go into the house. Your mum rang me on my mobile, Chloe – she's coming to get you and Erin.'

The dry earth of the track that led to the bottom field where Kestrel and Magpie were had turned to slippery mud. The girls started to run, but the storm suddenly broke. A flash of lightning forked across the sky. It was followed a few seconds later by a loud thunderclap.

Magpie whinnied in alarm; he was standing under a tree by the gate. Kestrel was cantering around the field, his head high. 'Here, boy,' called Erin, leaving Chloe to get Magpie.

Kestrel didn't seem to see her. His eyes were wide and scared. 'Kestrel!' Erin shouted, but her voice was whipped away by the wind. 'Kestrel! Come here!'

Chloe was struggling to get the gate open. Erin went to help her, hoping that if Kestrel realized Magpie was going, he would come over.

'I'll take Mags in, Erin!' shouted Chloe.

Erin nodded. Seeing Chloe leading Magpie through the gate, Kestrel gave a shrieking whinny and started cantering towards them. Erin quickly pulled the gate shut so he couldn't get out on his own.

There was a bright white flash as lightning forked down. Erin screamed as it hit the tree beside the gate. There was a loud bang as the tree exploded. Instinctively she covered her head with her hands as branches filled the air. She heard Chloe shout her name and saw a huge burning bough falling straight towards her . . .

★

★ ★

CHAPTER

Four

The branch filled Erin's vision. Then
suddenly a grey shape cannoned into her,
knocking her to one side. She landed a
metre away, sprawling on the muddy
ground.

'Kestrel!' she screamed as the grey pony
shied to avoid the enormous branch
himself. It thumped into the grass, missing
him by centimetres. Losing his footing in
the slippery mud, Kestrel crashed into the
fence and fell to the ground. Erin

scrambled to her feet, numb with fear. Kestrel tried to get up, but, as he thrashed around, one of his hind legs tangled in the thick orange rope that was tied tautly between the fence posts. The more he struggled the tighter the rope pulled, cutting into the skin on his leg.

'Steady, boy, steady!' Erin gasped.

Magpie had got free from Chloe and was galloping up the track in the direction of the yard. Chloe came running towards the gate, her eyes widening as she saw what had happened to Kestrel.

'Chloe, get a knife!' Erin yelled, her eyes never leaving Kestrel. 'Fetch Jackie!'

Chloe turned and ran as fast as she could back to the stables.

Heart pounding, but feeling an inner core of icy calm, Erin moved closer to

the terrified pony. She had to calm him
down. 'Steady, boy,' she soothed, trying to
avoid his kicking hooves. 'It's OK. I'm
here.' At the sound of her voice Kestrel's
wild movements slowed slightly. He
swung his head to look at her, his dark
eyes wide and scared, and then struggled
some more. Erin knew she mustn't move
too fast in case it startled him. She walked
forward, talking the whole time. 'There,'
she said, as he stopped again. She crouched
slowly down beside his neck. 'Shh,' she
murmured, hardly daring to look at the
rope wrapped round his leg. 'It's OK,' she
said, stroking him. 'We'll get you free.'

Within a few minutes, Chloe and
Jackie came running to the field. Jackie
gestured to Chloe that she should stay
back. 'I'm going to cut his leg free,' she

said quickly to Erin as she approached the grey pony. 'Keep talking to him, Erin. You're doing a great job.'

Kestrel's eyes widened as Jackie walked round to the fence. Erin stroked his face, pushing back his long mane. Jackie bent down and moved swiftly, pulling a knife out of her pocket and cutting the rope by the fence so Kestrel's leg came free. Then Jackie jumped out of the way, grabbing Erin and pulling her back as the pony threw himself over on to his side in relief and got to his feet, holding his injured leg off the ground.

'This looks bad,' said Jackie grimly, rain streaming down her face as she looked at the deep rope wound above Kestrel's hock. 'Let's get him inside.'

*

Jackie, Chloe and Erin stood in a stable
with Kestrel. The girls had rubbed him
down with wisps and then put a sweat
sheet on him to keep him warm, but his
coat was still soaking from the rain. He
was pulling at a haynet. He didn't seem
too upset about his leg, but Jackie was
worried because it was a very deep
wound. She'd called the vet, but the roads
were flooded and he had warned her that
it would be a while before he could get

there. Nicky had rung up on her mobile and said she couldn't get to the stables because of fallen trees. Jackie had suggested she go home and come back when the storm had blown itself out.

Now Jackie glanced out of the stable window. The thunder and lightning had stopped and the wind seemed to be dying down. 'Why don't we go back to the house and get dry?' she suggested.

Erin shook her head. 'I want to stay here with Kestrel.'

'OK,' Jackie said. 'But I'll go and get you both a hot chocolate.'

Jackie left the stable.

'Oh, Kestrel,' sighed Erin, burying her face in the grey pony's neck and hugging him.

Chloe looked out over the door. 'That

storm was awful. It's a total mess out
there.'

Erin joined her. It looked like a
hurricane had swept through the yard.
Brooms and spades had been whirled up
and dropped here and there, the hanging
baskets that usually decorated the stables
had fallen down, tiles had been pulled off
the roof and one of the field fences had
collapsed. A horrible thought struck her.
'I hope Tor and Mistral are OK.'

'They should be, shouldn't they?'
Chloe said.

They looked at each other uncertainly.
Erin reached for the hair on her
watchstrap. 'Keep a lookout for Jackie. I'll
try to speak to Tor and check.'

Chloe nodded.

Erin held the hair in her fingers. 'Tor,'

she called in her mind. 'Tor, are you
there? Can you hear me?'

'Erin.'

Erin felt a wave of relief as she heard
the stallion's voice in her head. 'Are you
all right?'

'Yes. Do not worry. The woods are
damaged, but Mistral and I turned
ourselves into our cloud forms and merged
with the winds in the skies. We are back in
the woods now. How are you and Chloe?'

'We're OK, but Kestrel's been injured.
Oh, Tor. Marianne's done so much
damage with the storm.'

'I know,' said Tor. 'And if she is allowed
to linger in the sky, there will be much
more damage, loss of life . . .'

'Erin!' Chloe said urgently. 'Jackie's
coming.'

'I've got to go,' Erin told Tor.

'Come tonight. As soon as you can.'

'We will,' promised Erin. She looked at Chloe in relief, warm inside from having spoken to the sky stallion. 'They're fine,' she said.

The stable door opened and Jackie came in. She was carrying two cans of Coke, a packet of biscuits and two spare fleece jackets. 'Sorry, girls, no electricity means no hot chocolate. The radio's saying a tornado swept through the town. Cars have been overturned, roofs have come off houses, the electricity pylons have come down. Your street was quite badly hit, Erin.' Jackie went to the door. 'I'm going to check the other ponies are OK in the barn and then, if the rain goes away, I'll start tidying up.'

★

Nicky arrived to collect them a couple
of hours later. By that time the vet had
been. He had dressed the wound, given
Kestrel antibiotics and said he would call
in again the next day.

'The girls have been fantastic,' Jackie
said to Nicky. 'They've been such a good
help all day and they were amazing in the
storm.' She told Nicky what had
happened with Kestrel. 'If Erin hadn't

kept calm, Kestrel could have panicked and done even more damage to himself.' She looked at Erin. 'You should be very proud of yourself, Erin.'

Erin glowed. She had only acted instinctively, but it was lovely being praised.

'You've both been great today, girls,' Jackie went on. 'Thanks for all your hard work. See you tomorrow.'

They got into the car. 'There's been some bad news, I'm afraid,' Nicky said.

'What?' asked Chloe anxiously.

'Xanthe and Allegra were in a car accident. The car skidded off the road in the rain. They're OK,' Nicky said quickly as both girls caught their breath. 'But Xanthe has broken her ankle.'

'Oh, poor Xanthe!' Chloe exclaimed.

'Let's just be thankful they weren't more badly hurt,' said Nicky. 'I spoke to her and she sent her love and said she is really sorry not to be able to come. She said she'd give you a ring.'

Erin and Chloe exchanged glances. No Xanthe. They were on their own. Erin felt sick. She looked out of the window at the devastation left by the storm. Fences had been blown down, cars overturned, trees uprooted.

'It's awful,' Erin said, looking round.

'It's worse here in Egglestone and back in Long Medlow than anywhere else on the coast,' said Nicky. 'It seems we were in the eye of the storm.' She glanced back at Erin. 'There was a bit more bad news actually.'

'More?' echoed Erin in alarm.

'Yes. I had a phone call from your dad. Your house has been hit by a tree.'

'What?' Erin stared at her. She felt like an ice cube was running down her spine.

'It's done quite a bit of damage to Jake's room, but at least none of you were inside at the time.'

Kestrel . . . Xanthe . . . our house . . . Erin's thoughts whirled as she heard the faint echo of Marianne's cold voice inside her head: *if you try to stop me, you – and all those around you – will be very, very sorry.*

A cold wave washed over her. Had Marianne deliberately set out to target her and her family and friends? She looked at Chloe and could see that she was thinking the same thing.

When they got to Chloe's house, they hung back while Nicky went in.

'Oh, Chloe,' Erin whispered, feeling sick still. 'Do you think the things that happened here and with Xanthe, and at my house with the tree falling on the roof, happened because Marianne meant them to?'

Chloe bit her lip. 'I don't know.'

The enormity of it all swept over Erin. Panic clawed through her. 'What if there's another storm? What if something worse happens?' she demanded.

Chloe squeezed her hands. 'Don't worry. We'll stop Marianne before then. We will!'

Up in the skies, Marianne watched them through her hagstone. 'You'll stop me, will you?' She laughed coldly. 'Well, we'll see about that . . .'

CHAPTER
Five

Erin could hardly wait to reach the
woods that night. 'I'm so glad you're OK,'
she said to Tor and Mistral when she got
to the clearing.

'Storms cannot injure us,' said Tor,
walking over and nuzzling her shoulder.

'What happened to you?' Mistral asked,
his eyes anxious.

Erin told the sky horses about the day.
'I wish Kestrel wasn't hurt.'

Tor snorted. 'As a weather weaver you

can use hagstones for healing. You could help him, Erin.'

'How?' asked Erin quickly.

'Find a healing stone among the pile of hagstones over there.' Tor looked across the clearing to where there was the pile of stones that Erin and Chloe had used to make the weather-weaving circle the night before. 'A healing stone has many holes in it.'

Erin quickly fetched a stone with five small holes. 'Won't my magic be too weak?' she said uncertainly.

'No. Just as with the seeing stones, the power for healing comes from the stone itself. You can free its power as you free a seeing stone's power. Hold it in your hands and let your mind empty. As the magic flows from you to the stone, imagine it healing wounds, making injuries better.' Tor moved closer to Erin, who had knelt down on the floor. 'The more vividly you can imagine the healing, the stronger the stone's healing powers will be.'

Determination flooded through Erin. She wasn't going to let Tor down. Looking at the stone, she allowed her mind to empty. She let her magic begin to flow into the stone, freeing its power . . .

'Hi!'

Erin jumped, dropping the stone as Chloe came flying into the clearing.

'Chloe!' exclaimed Erin. 'I was concentrating! I'm trying to use a healing stone.'

'Sorry,' Chloe apologized.

Erin forced a smile. 'It's OK. I didn't mean to snap. I just really want to learn to heal so I can help Kestrel.'

'That *would* be brilliant.' Chloe moved over to Mistral. 'I'll watch from over here.'

But as Erin picked the stone up and started trying to concentrate again she was aware of Chloe stroking Mistral and whispering to him. Every time she tried to empty her mind and focus on the stone the noises would drag her back.

'I can't concentrate!' she said,
frustration making her voice cross. She
threw a sharp look at Chloe. 'Can you
be quiet?'

Chloe looked taken aback.

'Perhaps you could go with Mistral to
see if you can find an animal who is
injured, Chloe,' suggested Tor softly.
'Then when Erin does free the stone's
power, she can use it.'

'Sure.' Chloe shrugged.

Mistral and Chloe set off together
through the trees. Tor breathed gently on
Erin's skin. She smiled quickly at him.
'OK, I'll try again.' She cleared her mind
and felt magic flow from her fingers into
the stone. Over and over again she
thought healing thoughts. The stone
grew warm then cold. She glanced at Tor

hopefully. 'It's gone cold. I think it might have worked.'

Just then Chloe returned. She had a young mistle thrush nestling in her hands. 'I've found a bird that's hurt its wing.'

Tor pushed Erin gently with his nose. 'Try the stone, Erin. Hold it close to the thrush's wing.'

Erin looked at the young bird with its brown feathers and pale, speckled chest. 'Hey, there,' she said soothingly. The bird opened its mouth and chirruped.

Erin gently touched the stone to the bird's injured wing. She felt the stone grow warm. The bird shifted slightly.

'Has it worked?' Chloe whispered.

'I don't know,' admitted Erin.

Chloe put the thrush on the ground. It lifted its wings up and tried to flap, but it couldn't quite lift its injured wing high enough.

'Oh,' said Erin in disappointment.

'It's looking lots better though,' said Chloe. 'It couldn't move its wing at all when I found it.' She looked impressed. 'That's really cool, Erin!'

'Not cool enough,' sighed Erin.

'You just need to practise some more,' Tor reassured her. 'When the stone has been used once you must then use your magic to call forth its powers again.'

Erin spent the rest of the evening trying to make the stone powerful enough to heal properly. Chloe got bored with hanging around and set off to find more animals to be helped. By the end of the evening Erin had got the stone working well enough to heal the thrush, a stoat with a damaged tail, a rabbit with a large cut and an owl who also had an injured wing.

'Can I go and try on Kestrel?' Erin said eagerly.

'Tomorrow,' Tor told her. He saw her face fall. 'I know you want to go now, but it is late and it will be better to wait until you have practised using this magic more.'

A thought struck Erin. 'I wonder what Jackie will say if I do it though? How can I explain it?'

'Maybe it would be best if you simply quickened the healing process rather than leaving no trace of a wound,' suggested Tor.

Erin nodded. That made sense. Much as she wanted to make Kestrel completely better straight away, Jackie would be absolutely bewildered if Kestrel's wound suddenly closed up and healed.

'We should go,' said Chloe, glancing at the sky. 'The night's almost over.'

Erin realized that Chloe must have had a rather dull time. 'I'm sorry we don't ever seem to get the chance to do any normal stardust magic at the moment.'

'Don't worry,' said Chloe, rolling her eyes. 'I'm used to it.'

Erin hoped she wasn't really upset with her. 'Come on,' she said. 'We'd better go. We can play tag on the way home though.'

Chloe smiled. 'OK!'

Calling goodbye to the horses, the two girls flew away, chasing each other across the skies.

Up in the clouds, Marianne looked down and smiled . . .

CHAPTER

Six

Oh, Mum. It was really difficult last night. I was trying to do healing magic, but I couldn't do it properly. It kept almost working, but not enough. Tor said I was doing well, but I need to be able to do it well enough to make Kestrel's leg better. And I'm sure Chloe's a bit fed up with me. She didn't get to do much last night. I feel bad about that. I know she wishes she could do weather-weaving magic and she finds it hard that it's just me who can do it, but I had to keep practising. I just wanted to

*get the magic right so I could help Kestrel. I
hope she understands.*

Erin sighed and put down her pen. She
could see the sun rising in the sky
through her half-open curtains. It was
early in the morning and no one else was
up yet, but she hadn't slept well. She
wanted to be able to heal Kestrel so badly.
Now, she picked up a hagstone. Would
she be able to make it work well enough
that night?

Turning it over in her hands, she felt a
tingling feeling. Excitement leapt
through her like a flame flaring. Magic!
The stone must be trying to show her
something again.

Eagerly, she stared at the hole and let
her mind go blank, trusting to the magic

just as Tor had once told her to. To her
surprise, a vision of Chloe appeared –
Chloe writing in a diary. Erin stared. She
hadn't even known Chloe *had* a diary!
Chloe was frowning. The vision seemed to
zoom in on the words. Erin caught sight
of her own name:

Erin was really annoying last night . . .

Erin felt a jolt. She forced her eyes away.
It was Chloe's private diary. She knew she
shouldn't read it, but she couldn't stop
herself. Her gaze flicked back.

*All she did was her weather magic. We
didn't get to do anything fun. And she wasn't
even that good at healing. She wants to heal
Kestrel, but I don't think she'll be able to.*

Erin's heart thudded. Chloe hadn't said
that to her! She'd been really
encouraging.

She thinks we'll stop Marianne too, Chloe's writing went on. *But I don't know how. She's got no power. We'll never be able to stop a dark spirit like Marianne.*

Erin blinked and felt the vision fade.

A sick feeling rose inside her. She should never have read the diary even if it was in a vision. But it was horrible to know that Chloe thought those things about her.

Trying to push what she had seen from her mind, she got up and went downstairs.

Chloe came hurrying to meet Erin at the stables that day. 'Hi!' she said cheerfully. She dropped her voice. 'I mailed Xanthe to see how she is and told her what's been happening. I said about how you need to find a way to increase your power so you can send images of Tor to the clouds and destroy the dark gateway. I hope she can help.'

Erin nodded, feeling very awkward. It was strange having Chloe chat so normally and yet knowing what was really going on in her head. For a moment she wondered if she should say anything, but that would mean admitting she had been spying on Chloe. She decided to keep quiet.

'I hope you can make the stone work tonight,' Chloe went on. 'I bet you'll be able to.'

'Mmm,' Erin said.

At that moment – to her relief – Anna, one of the other helpers, arrived. Chloe changed the subject.

'Should we go and see Kestrel, Erin?'

Erin nodded.

'It's going to be horrible for you not being able to ride him,' chatted Chloe as they walked towards the stables. 'Do you want a ride on Ziggy later?'

Erin nodded again, but didn't speak.

Chloe frowned. 'Are you OK? You're being really quiet.'

'I'm . . . I'm fine,' Erin muttered.

Chloe smiled at her sympathetically. 'If

you're worried about the healing, don't be. I know you'll be able to do it.' She reached out to squeeze Erin's hand. Erin flinched and moved quickly away, hurrying the last few metres to Kestrel's stable. He was standing listlessly, his head hanging low.

'Hey, boy,' Erin said, grateful to have him to concentrate on. Chloe was being so nice it was hard to believe what she had written. Kestrel lifted his head and pricked his ears, but didn't move. She went in and checked his leg. The area around the bandage was warm and looked very swollen.

'How is it?' asked Chloe.

Just then, Jackie looked over the door. 'Hi, girls. Kestrel's not looking too great today. The vet's coming back later. Could you two start by mucking out the barn?

Fran and Katie are here too and they've just started on it.'

Jackie hurried away.

'Oh, great,' Erin groaned. Mucking out with Fran and Katie was not her idea of fun.

Fran and Katie were both in the barn. Erin tried to ignore them. It was fairly easy. They seemed far more interested in talking to Chloe than her. They hadn't been at the stables for a few days so they had only just found out she'd got Ziggy for her birthday.

'He's really gorgeous,' said Fran. 'Can I have a ride on him later?'

'Yeah, I guess,' Chloe said reluctantly.

'You're so lucky,' said Katie enviously. 'I'd love my own pony.'

'When are you going to ride him?' Fran asked.

'Probably once we've finished mucking out. I'll ask Jackie if it's OK.'

'Cool!' said Fran. 'We'll help you groom him, Chloe.'

Erin stabbed her fork into the straw bed. Fran and Katie were never usually friendly with Chloe. It was so obvious they were only being like that because they wanted to ride Ziggy.

When the stalls in the barn were all mucked out and clean straw had been put down, Chloe turned to Erin. 'Shall we go and catch Ziggy?'

'I'll come with you,' called Fran eagerly.

'And me,' said Katie.

Chloe looked at Erin.

'It won't take four of us,' said Fran pointedly.

'I think I'll go and check on Kestrel,' Erin said, tight-lipped.

Chloe groomed with Fran and Katie and then rode Ziggy and let them each have a go on him. Erin stayed away. After grooming Kestrel, she held him while the vet came and redressed his leg and gave him another injection, and then she started grooming the other ponies. She didn't see Chloe again until just before lunch when Jackie asked them both to sweep the yard.

'You should have come and had a ride on Ziggy,' Chloe said to her. 'Why didn't you?'

Erin shrugged and didn't say anything.

Chloe looked at her. 'Look, if you're mad about Fran and Katie hanging around, I'm sorry,' she said in a low voice.

'There wasn't much I could do. You know I'd rather have been riding and grooming with you, Erin.'

Erin felt a rush of relief and her bad mood started to fade. She smiled. 'That's OK. It was good to spend some time with Kestrel anyway.'

'Should we go and eat lunch round the back of the barn where they can't find us?' said Chloe.

Erin grinned at her. 'Yeah, let's!'

When Erin got home she went into her bedroom and shut the door. Her brothers had all just got back and the house was filled with noise again as they inspected the damage the tree had done to Jake's room. Erin went to the window and pulled out the hair from her watchstrap.

'Tor?' She wasn't sure why she was calling him. She just wanted to hear his voice. She knew deep down she was still shaken up at finding out that Chloe didn't believe she would be able to heal Kestrel or that they would defeat Marianne.

'I am here.'

Erin felt the rush of happiness she always felt when Tor spoke to her. 'How are you?' she asked.

'Worried. I can feel my herd's distress. I wish I could go through the hidden gateway and chase the dark one out of the skies. If only the gateway was not so hard to use . . .'

Erin heard the frustration in the stallion's voice.

'I can feel another storm coming,' he went on. 'And with your powers being so weak, we will be unable to stop it, Erin.'

'If only there was some way to increase my power,' said Erin. 'I wonder if Chloe has heard from Xanthe yet? I'll ask her tonight. I'll be with you as soon as I can.'

'I will see you then,' said Tor.

Erin looked down at the stone again. Almost immediately the darkness in the centre seemed to flicker and grow. She stared. Was the stone trying to show her another vision? Yes. She started to see a picture. It was Chloe again! She was sitting at her desk, writing in her diary.

No, this time I am not going to read what she's writing, Erin thought, but the words in the open diary seemed to jump out at her before she could look away:

It was really fun today. Fran and Katie helped me with Ziggy. Erin was in a mood about that. But that's just because she was jealous. I had a good time. I hope I get to see them tomorrow.

Erin felt like she'd been hit. *That wasn't what Chloe had said. She must have been lying to me*, Erin realized. The vision disappeared.

Erin put the stone down. Her fingers were shaking. So Chloe was looking forward to seeing Fran and Katie the

next day. She'd had a really good time
with them, had she?

Pain stabbed through Erin. She
couldn't believe Chloe had written that.
Her whole world suddenly felt shaky and
unsafe. Chloe was supposed to be her best
friend. She looked at the hair in the strap
of her watch. For a moment she longed to
talk to Tor again, to have the comfort of
his warm voice. But what would she say
to him? This was just about her and
Chloe. Not about magic at all.

Erin sank down on her bed. It was
horrible knowing Chloe was saying one
thing and thinking another all the time.
She covered her face with her hands and
took a deep breath. All of a sudden, she
felt very, very alone.

CHAPTER

Seven

Erin sat on the ground in the woods,
staring at the healing stone in her
hands. Drizzle fell around her, but she
hardly noticed. She imagined wounds
closing up, bones mending, blood
vanishing from cuts. Her fingers felt
as if they were buzzing. She
concentrated as hard as she could. She
wanted the stone to be as powerful as
possible. For a moment it burnt so red-
hot that she almost dropped it, but

almost immediately it turned as cold as ice.

Erin glanced up. Tor was standing just in front of her. Chloe and Mistral were behind him. They were all watching.
'I think it's ready.' She avoided Chloe's eyes. She had got to the clearing first again and hadn't really spoken to Chloe since she'd arrived. 'The stone's really freezing.'

'The colder it is, the more powerful its magic will be,' Tor told her.

'I'll go and try it on Kestrel,' said Erin eagerly. She flew into the air. Chloe followed her. 'I'll go on my own,' Erin said.

Chloe looked at her in surprise. 'Don't be silly.'

'Oh, I'm silly now as well as jealous,

am I?' Erin couldn't resist muttering. She
flew off fast through the drizzling rain.

'What?' Chloe hurried to catch up
with her.

Erin shook her head as if to say it
didn't matter.

'What's up with you, Erin?' Chloe asked.

'Forget it,' replied Erin.

Chloe frowned. 'You're in a seriously
weird mood tonight!'

Erin ignored her and flew on. She

wanted to see if she could heal Kestrel. That was all that mattered.

Kestrel started as the door opened. Erin quickly let her camouflage drop. As soon as he saw her, he relaxed and whinnied softly. She went forward and gave him a hug. He looked curious, but not alarmed at the night-time visit. 'I'm going to try and make you better,' Erin told him, glad to be able to block out Chloe for a moment by concentrating on the pony. She gently put a hand on the skin above his bandage. Despite the injection that day, it was still hot and swollen and he was keeping his weight off that leg. She took the healing stone out of her pocket.

'Do you want me to hold his head?' offered Chloe.

'It's OK. I can manage on my own,' Erin replied.

'You don't have to do everything on your own, you know,' Chloe said in exasperation. 'Honestly, Erin, I can help with some things!'

Ignore her, Erin told herself, crouching down. She murmured quietly to Kestrel and placed the stone above the wound. Kestrel flinched, but then she felt him start to relax. Slowly, she moved the cold stone around the hot, swollen part of his leg. She brushed it over the bandage and then held it lightly where she knew the wound was. The stone tingled under her fingers. She closed her eyes, imagining all the healing thoughts she'd had when she had tried to free the power in the stone. She pictured Kestrel's wound under the bandage. She imagined it slowly healing inside, leaving just a scar. She didn't know how long she sat there for, but slowly she felt the stone start to lose its icy coldness. When it felt just like any normal stone, she straightened up. 'Its magic is used up,' she said. She gently touched the skin around the bandage. It felt much cooler and the swelling seemed to have gone down. 'I think it might have worked.'

'I suppose we'd better not take the bandage off to look,' said Chloe. 'We might not be able to get it on again.'

That made sense even though, just then, Erin didn't feel like admitting anything Chloe said might be useful.

Kestrel rubbed Erin's arm with his head. She was sure his eyes looked brighter.

'We'd better get back to Tor.' Erin
hugged Kestrel goodbye. 'See you
tomorrow after school,' she promised him.

'That was really good,' said Chloe,
looking genuinely impressed as they left.
'I'm so glad you could help.'

Erin felt a small flare of triumph.
Chloe should never have doubted her.

'You know, while you were healing
Kestrel, I was thinking about the

prophecy,' Chloe went on. 'About the last
verse especially.' She recited it:

> *'Yet danger is found with the new*
> *   gateway –*
> *Beware the dark horse who leaps for*
> *   the sky.*
> *With arrow of fire and grey feather's*
> *   direction,*
> *Two must help here or all hopes will die.*
> *If the darkest impostor is not defeated,*
> *Then never again will the cloud stallion*
> *   fly.'*

'*Two must help here*,' Chloe repeated. 'I bet
that means us. That we both have to help.'
    'Mmm, it might do,' said Erin.
    'The darkest impostor must be
Marianne,' said Chloe. 'But what does it

mean about an arrow of fire and a grey
feather? I was wondering if the arrow of
fire might have something to do with
me. After all, I can make arrows of fire
with my summer magic.'

'It probably means lightning or
something like that,' Erin said.

'But it *could* mean me,' persisted
Chloe.

'How could arrows of fire help? I bet

it doesn't mean you,' said Erin, shaking her head.

Chloe frowned. 'Oh, why? Because it's always got to be you? Is that it? You want to do it all yourself.'

'Of course not. I –' said Erin in astonishment.

Chloe didn't let her finish. Temper flared in her eyes. 'It's always all about your weather-weaving powers at the moment, isn't it, Erin? *You* doing stuff with Tor. *You* seeing Marianne. *You* healing Kestrel. Well, the prophecy says *two can help*. And that means it's not just you in this, Erin. *I'm* important too. You'll see!'

She turned and flew off, tears in her eyes.

'Chloe, wait!' Erin was completely taken aback by Chloe's outburst. She looked all around, but Chloe had gone.

CHAPTER

Eight

Dear Mum,
It's been a weird night. Good in some ways.
Bad in others. There's no news from Xanthe,
and Chloe and I had an argument because
she's been feeling left out. She thinks the
prophecy says something about her, but I don't
think it is her. When I said that, she got mad
and lost her temper. I guess I should have
noticed that she's been feeling a bit cross about
stuff, but I've just been so busy thinking about
everything else. We never seem to be able to

use the hidden gateway and Tor thinks there's another storm coming, but we can't stop it because my powers are too weak. I really wish there was something I could do.

Erin didn't want to write more – she didn't want to think about how frustrating everything felt. Instead she picked up her mum's diary and turned to 20 June, today's date, wondering what her mum had been doing on the same day when she had been eleven.

Mum and I are going to seal the gateways again tomorrow. We have all the things we need. I can't wait!

Erin quickly turned the page and looked at the next entry. Every seven years, her

granny and then her mum had performed
a spell to seal the gateways to the cloud
kingdom so that no one could pass
between the worlds. The spell had run
out last year, almost seven years after her
mum had died. She read on.

Mum and I went to the giant hagstone
gateway first. She held a seeing stone in the
centre of the gateway, put it into the silver

bowl and then she brushed air over it with the grey feather . . .

Erin broke off. *A grey feather!* Was that the same grey feather that the prophecy had mentioned – a grey feather to seal a gateway? Was it a special grey feather or would any grey feather work? Her eyes skimmed quickly over the rest of the words.

Then she dropped water on it from the bottle, passed it over the candle flame in the bowl and then covered the hole in the stone up with earth from the jar. The spell uses the four stardust elements – air, earth, water and fire – and mixes them with hagstone magic. After she'd done everything, she held the seeing stone in the gateway again and said, 'Be sealed.' The air inside the gateway seemed to shiver and then that was it . . .

Erin reread the entry several times. She wished her mum had written more, but that was all there was. Turning her light off, she tried to go to sleep, but she couldn't stop thinking about the grey feather and the prophecy. She reached under her pillow, her fingers instinctively curling round the hagstone underneath it. Her hand started to tingle.

She pulled the hagstone out and looked at it in the darkness. The hole was growing and she could see a picture. A study with a large desk. There were shelves around the room, a dark bureau with hagstones on it in one corner and a table covered with a mixture of objects in another. Goosebumps ran up her arms. She knew this place. It was Marianne's study in her house on the cliff top. It was the house that had once belonged to Erin's grandmother. When Marianne had bought the house, called Lookout Point, Erin had had no idea that Marianne was her great-grandmother's sister.

She wondered why she was seeing the room. She knew Tor said she had to trust in her visions, it was the stones helping her, but sometimes they could be very confusing!

And then her eyes fell on something. *A grey feather!* It was on the tabletop. Suddenly it all came flooding back to Erin. Of course, she'd seen it when she'd been in Marianne's study one night. On the table there was a silver bowl, a glass bottle, a small pot of earth, a candle and a grey feather! All the things that her mum said were needed for sealing a gateway.

The vision started to fade. Erin blinked and found herself back in her bedroom again. She gripped the stone hard. She knew where to find the grey feather now. But how was she was going to get it and what was she going to do with it if she did get it? And why did Marianne have all the things to seal a gateway when she had always been trying to create one?

Erin stared at the ceiling, thinking about it all.

Erin was still thinking about the grey feather when she got to the stables that day. Jo had given her a lift after school to save her cycling. Rain was drizzling down. 'I heard on the news that another storm is likely to break this afternoon or evening,' Jo said. 'If the weather gets worse, I'll come and get you – otherwise I'll collect you at six. Your dad and I thought we would take you out for a Chinese tonight.'

'Cool,' said Erin in surprise. She loved Chinese food, but they only usually went out as a special treat. 'Why are we going out?'

Jo smiled. 'You'll find out this evening!'

As she got out of the car, Chloe arrived. The two of them looked at each other across the car park. Erin hesitated, remembering the argument, but she was desperate to share her vision about the feather. Taking a deep breath, she started walking towards Chloe.

But just then Fran and Katie came jogging down from the yard.

'Hi, Chloe!' they called, going over to her. They ignored Erin.

'Oh, hi,' Chloe said.

'Can we help you with Ziggy again today?' Katie asked eagerly.

'It was really good fun yesterday,' said Fran, linking arms with Chloe.

Her words pierced straight into Erin's brain. She swung round on her heel and half ran to Kestrel's stable, wanting just to give him a hug. But Jackie was there.

'Hi, Erin,' she said.

'How's Kestrel's leg?' Erin asked hopefully.

'Well, I can hardly believe it, but it's loads better. Look!'

Erin came into the stable. Jackie had

taken the bandage off. For a moment Erin forgot about Chloe and her heart rose. The swelling had completely gone and the sides of the wound had closed together. There was still a mark there, but it looked as if it was healing really well. 'I've never known a wound heal so quickly,' said Jackie. 'The vet came over today. He couldn't believe it either. It's fantastic though.' She patted Kestrel. 'He's not even lame now.'

She left the stable. Erin put her arms round Kestrel's neck. 'I'm so glad you're better.' He nuzzled her. Hearing voices, Erin went to Kestrel's door and looked out. Chloe was walking down to the field with Fran and Katie. As she passed Kestrel's door, Chloe looked over towards it. For a moment she seemed to hesitate. Erin's fingers tightened on Kestrel's mane.

Please stop, she thought. But then Fran
said something to Chloe and they
laughed and walked on by.

Erin spent the afternoon on her own.
When she went into the tack room to
get Kestrel's grooming kit, Fran and Katie
were there without Chloe. Fran stuck her
leg out and Erin stumbled over it.

'Have a good trip!' Fran smirked and
Katie giggled.

'Come on,' said Fran to Katie. 'Let's go and find Chloe.'

As the time passed, Erin got more miserable and the rain got heavier. The fields were waterlogged and water flowed from them on to the yard. The girls put sandbags outside the stable doors to try to stop water flooding in and soaking the horses' beds. Soon they were all sloshing around in ten centimetres of water and Jackie said that she thought they should all go home.

'The roads are starting to flood. Do you want to give your parents a ring and see if they can collect you early?'

As Erin sat on the bench in the tack room waiting for Jo to arrive, unease shivered through her. The storm was

definitely coming. Chloe, Fran and Katie
hurried up the yard from Ziggy's stable.
Their heads were bent against the wind
and rain.

Chloe's eyes met Erin's. She looked
worried.

Erin turned away.

'Ooh, there's a funny smell in here,'
said Fran, wrinkling her nose and
looking pointedly at Erin as she came
into the tack room.

Erin tried to ignore her. She knew
Fran was just trying to get her to react. It
was pouring down outside and she didn't
want to have to wait in the rain, but she
didn't want to be in the tack room with
Fran and Katie either.

'I want to sit there,' said Fran, hands on
her hips. 'Move, Erin.' She frowned when

Erin didn't move. 'Didn't you hear what I said?'

Chloe opened her mouth, but Erin had had enough. She was upset over Chloe, worried about the storm and scared about what Marianne might do. She had magic powers, even if she couldn't use them properly at the moment. Why should she have to put up with Fran and her dumb comments any longer? Her temper snapped. 'I heard, but I'll move when I want to!'

Fran couldn't have looked more shocked if the tack-trunk in the corner had started talking.

'Just leave me alone,' Erin went on, anger beating through her, hot and strong. 'You're a bully. You think you're so great, but the only friend you've got is

Katie. Chloe doesn't really like you. You just go around acting like you're cool. Well, you're so not!'

Fran's mouth gaped open.

Katie's eyes were wide.

'So you don't want to be friends with me, well that's fine,' Erin went on. 'I don't want to be friends with you either. But

I'm fed up with all your comments and the stuff you do. If you don't stop, I'm going to tell Jackie.'

'You wouldn't say anything,' Fran said, but Erin heard the slight tremor in her voice.

'Want to bet!' Erin lifted her chin and stood up. 'You can sit down now, but only because *I* don't want to any more!' She marched out of the tack room. The rain fell on her heated face, little spots of cold, but she didn't care. She felt as if a huge weight had lifted from her shoulders. For months now, she'd put up with Fran getting at her – *I did it!* she thought. *I really did it. I stood up to her!*

'Erin!' She heard Chloe calling her, heard her feet splashing through the puddles.

But Erin didn't want to speak to her.
To her relief, she saw Jo's car pull into the
car park. She broke into a jog and,
ignoring Chloe's shouts, ran to meet her
stepmum. Jumping into the car, she
pulled the door shut.

'Hi,' said Jo.

'Hi,' said Erin, her heart beating fast.

She looked out through the rain-
covered window. Chloe was standing in
the car park, staring after her as Jo drove
away.

CHAPTER

Nine

'What did you say?' Erin stared at her dad and Jo, who were sitting across the table. Around them there was the sound of waiters bustling about, people talking and faint music playing. But Erin felt it all fade away. All she could think about was what her dad had just said. 'I'm getting Kestrel? He's going to be *mine*?'

Erin's dad nodded. 'Jackie rang us up to say she wasn't sure he was cut out to be a riding-school pony and she'd noticed what a bond you had with him . . .'

'And she said how dedicated you are and what a good help and how responsible you are with the ponies,' Jo added. 'And she asked us if we would be interested in having him on loan. That means we pay for him and you look after and ride him as if he was your very own pony.'

Her dad nodded. 'We've felt for a while that it does seem unfair the boys get to do all the things they want with their tennis and wind-surfing and sailing, and you don't have anything like that. So we thought, why not?'

Erin stared at them, dumbstruck. When Jo had suggested going out for a meal, Erin had never in a million years suspected they would say something like this.

'Are you pleased?' asked Jo eagerly.

'Pleased' didn't begin to describe how Erin felt. It was as if she had fireworks going off throughout her whole body.

'Oh, thank you! Thank you! Thank you!' She jumped up from the table and raced round to hug them both. For a minute, the storm, Marianne and all her worries vanished from her mind. She knew that other people in the restaurant were looking at her curiously, but for once she didn't care at all! Kestrel was going to be her pony – really and truly hers. He might be on loan, but no one else would ride him or look after him.

'So I'll take it that you *are* pleased,' her dad said.

Erin gave him the biggest beam possible in reply.

★

When Erin got home she almost phoned Chloe, but she felt awkward and decided not to. *I'll tell her tonight*, she thought.

The weather forecasters were predicting more storms. '*People are being advised to stay indoors*,' the TV weatherman said. '*Gusts of up to a hundred miles an hour are possible and torrential rain is likely, particularly along the coast.*'

Erin went upstairs feeling her joy at finding out about Kestrel fading slightly. She picked a hagstone up from her window ledge. If only she could help Tor and do something about the storms.

She looked at the stone. 'Show me something that might help,' she pleaded.

The darkness of the hole began to grow. Erin caught her breath. What was she going to see?

She saw a house. Lookout Point. Marianne's house. But it looked different. There were pots of flowers round the door and brightly checked blue curtains hanging in the windows. Erin felt herself moving closer until she had entered the vision and was at the open front door. She looked inside. A woman was standing on the staircase in a flowery dress and an apron. She looked about sixty; her long hair was tied back in a bun and her blue eyes were clear and sharp in her familiar heart-shaped face.

Great-grandmother Margaret! Erin realized with a start, recognizing her great-grandmother from old photos she had seen.

Her great-grandmother looked at her and Erin had the feeling she knew she was there. She turned and walked up the

stairs. Erin followed. They went up two
flights of stairs and then into an attic. It
was in the eaves of the roof and had
boxes stored on both sides.

Margaret walked to the end and then, to
Erin's surprise, she undid her bun. Her
grey hair tumbled down her back.
Margaret took a pair of golden embroidery
scissors and an envelope from the pocket
of her apron, cut off a lock of hair and put

it into the envelope. She folded it over and tucked it into a crack at the base of one of the beams. Then she turned and looked at Erin.

The vision began to fade. The last image Erin had was of her great-grandmother smiling at her.

She blinked and realized she was back in her bedroom. Excitement beat through her like wild fire. Would the hair still be there? If it was she could use it. Erin caught her breath. *If I could use Great-grandmother's hair to add her powers to mine, I wouldn't be weak any more!*

Erin closed her fingers round the hair in her wristwatch. 'Tor!'

'Yes, Erin?' said Tor.

'Oh, Tor,' Erin exclaimed. 'I've just had

a vision and I think I know where I can get some of my great-grandmother's hair!'

Tor whinnied in astonishment. 'Her hair! We could use that to give you power, all the power you could possibly need. Where is it?'

'Lookout Point. I'll go tonight. I've thought about it. It should be OK because Marianne's in the clouds.'

'You and Chloe must be careful,' Tor said, sounding worried. 'Come to the woods straight afterwards and call me if you are in any danger.'

'OK,' promised Erin, not wanting to admit she was planning on going without Chloe. 'I'll see you later, Tor!'

She put the stone down, her heart beating fast. If the hair was still there, then maybe, just maybe, they could defeat Marianne after all!

Erin flew towards Lookout Point with a bag on her back. She felt a bit silly but, knowing Chloe wouldn't be with her, she had brought her mum's diary with her for company. It was in her bag with her torch. She wished she hadn't argued with Chloe and that they could be going there together.

She reached the cliff tops and saw that the tide was out. If she could get the hair and use it to boost her power, then maybe she could clear the clouds blocking the moonlight just long enough for the gateway to form and for Tor to get through it.

As Erin approached the house, she heard a noise like a stifled cough. She

spun round, but the sky was empty. Her
skin prickled. She cursed herself for not
having camouflaged herself. She'd been
too busy thinking about what she had to
do.

'*Camouflagus*,' she whispered quickly.
Erin vanished against the sky and flew
on. But she felt spooked. She was sure
she had heard someone behind her.

Trying to tell herself she was just
imagining it, she reached the house. It was
dark and deserted. Erin flew round and
saw that one of the upstairs windows was
slightly open. She pushed it open a bit
more. It was just big enough for her to get
inside. As she scrambled in, she got the
torch out of her bag. Its yellow beam cut
through the darkness. Heart hammering,
she looked around and saw that she was in

a corridor. At the end she could see the stairs that led up to the attic.

Feeling almost faint with fear, Erin ran up them and pushed the attic door open. She tensed, half feeling that something was going to jump out or that she would see something horrible, but there was just a bare room. All the boxes that had been there when her great-grandmother had lived in the house had gone. Erin hurried

to the end of the room. She looked at the old beams, her heart leaping as she spotted a glint of paper in the crack underneath one. Could this be it? Could this be what she needed?

She carefully eased out an old yellowing envelope. Opening it, she saw a lock of grey hair.

Erin touched it in awe with a finger. She folded the envelope carefully back up and put it into her bag. She didn't know how they would use it, but she hoped Tor would. She thought about the study downstairs. The feather might be in it still. If it was, she could take it in case they needed it to destroy the gateway. *It'll be better to get it now than to come back later*, she reasoned, although she really just wanted to get out of there.

Shining the torch in front of her, she
went down the stairs. A floorboard
creaked and she jumped. Every nerve in
her body felt like it was on red alert.

She reached the study on the ground
floor. As she pushed open the door, her
skin started to prickle again. The air was
still and heavy, almost thick. It felt as if
Marianne had worked magic in this room.

The table still had the objects on it – a
silver bowl, a crystal bottle, a jar of earth,
a white candle and a grey feather. Erin
picked them all up and put them into her
bag, the feather last. She would need
them to seal the gateway if they ever did
defeat Marianne. As she lifted the feather
off the table, an icy gust suddenly blew
through the room and the study door
slammed shut with a bang. Erin jumped

about a foot in the air. She stared at the door. Where had that wind come from?

There was a faint crackling sound from behind her. She spun round. Ice was spreading over the windowpane. Another gust of freezing wind swirled about her and snowflakes began to appear around her ankles. What was happening?

She ran to the door and grabbed the handle to pull it open, but she jumped back with a cry. The metal was so cold that it seemed to burn her fingers and the whole door frame was iced up. Erin looked at the window again in panic. It was completely frosted over now and snow was settling on her hair and face. The air in the room was growing colder by the second.

It's a trap, Erin realized in horror. *There's no way out!*

CHAPTER
Ten

Panic clawed through Erin. She was going to freeze to death in here! Maybe Tor could help? She reached for the hair on her watchstrap, but it was brittle and frozen. 'Tor!' she exclaimed as a bit of it broke off in her fingers.

But there was no reply. Her heart plummeted. The magic trap was also stopping the hair from working.

She ran to the window. Maybe she could break it? She grabbed the silver bowl and banged it against the glass, but it was like hitting a sheet of metal. She could feel the cold in the room stealing over her, feel it sinking into her blood, chilling her, freezing her . . .

She looked at the window and screamed as she suddenly saw a face on the other side. The scream changed to a shriek as she realized who it was. 'Chloe!' she gasped.

'Erin!' shouted Chloe from outside. 'What are you doing in there? What's going on?'

'I'm trapped! There's a spell on the room. It's getting colder and colder. I can't get out!' Erin wondered what Chloe was doing out there, but there was no time to ask.

Chloe looked horrified. 'I'll come and help you. I'll get in through the window.'

'No, don't!' Erin was shivering
violently. 'There might be other traps! Go
and get Tor!'

'There isn't time,' said Chloe. 'I know!
My summer magic – I can use that!' She
lifted her hands. 'Fire be with me!' She
pointed at the window and concentrated
hard. Where she pointed, the ice started
to melt and turn to water. Chloe slowly
moved her hand across the window
frame, her fingers spreading open.

'It's working!' Erin cried through
numb lips, as the thick sheet of ice on the
window began to melt, running away as
rivulets of water.

Her teeth were chattering
uncontrollably. Her fingers were so cold
she could barely lift the window catch. She
fumbled with it, pushing it as hard as she

could. The window banged open and she felt the warm air of the summer night outside stream in. The next moment, Chloe was grabbing her hand and pulling her out of the freezing, snowy room.

'Oh, Erin!' Chloe flung her arms round her and hugged her as Erin collapsed in a heap on the ground, unable to do anything but shiver and rub her arms with her hands.

'Fire be with me,' Chloe murmured.

Erin felt a wave of warmth flow over her as Chloe moved her hand in front of her face and then down her body.

'Oh.' She breathed out in relief as her shivers faded. 'Thank you!'

Chloe clenched her hand and the magic was gone. 'What happened?' she demanded. 'Hang on. Is it safe for us to

be here? Is Marianne somewhere around?'

'No, she's not here. I'm sure she's still in the clouds. I think it was a trap. It started when I picked up this!' Erin pulled the grey feather out of her bag.

'The grey feather!' Chloe's eyes widened. 'What's going on?'

'I saw a vision. Two actually.' Erin told Chloe about the vision that had shown her the feather and the vision of her great-grandmother. 'I got the hair from the attic.' She took the envelope out of her bag. 'And then I went to get the feather, but as I picked it up the magic started.' She frowned. 'But what were you doing here?'

Chloe hesitated. 'I followed you. I was on my way to the woods when I saw you flying over the cliff top in this direction. I was camouflaged – as you should have been.'

'I forgot!' Erin admitted. 'But I'm very glad I did now. So *you* were the person following me.'

Chloe nodded. 'Yes. It was me. I wanted to see where you were going and what you were doing. I should just have said hello and let you see me.'

'It's lucky you didn't,' said Erin. 'Because then you would probably have been in there with me. Thank you so much for saving me.'

'I'm glad I could. Oh, Erin, I'm sorry we argued!' The words burst out of Chloe. 'I know I upset you a bit by spending time with Fran and Katie this afternoon. It's just that you've been in such a weird mood the last few days and haven't seemed to want me around and, well, I guess I have been feeling a bit left out because you've been doing so much magic and I haven't really been able to do anything. But I shouldn't have got mad yesterday. I've been wanting to say sorry all day. I should have done.'

'It's OK,' Erin said. 'It was a stupid argument. I should never have said that the prophecy doesn't mean you – no one knows what it means, so maybe it does. I should have realized you were feeling left out. It's just I've been so worried about Kestrel and ... well, I have been in a bit of a bad mood with you,' she admitted. She saw Chloe's frown and hesitated. But she knew what she had to do. It was going to be horrible, but she had to tell Chloe the truth about what she'd seen and sort it out.

'It was because I saw you writing in your diary. I didn't mean to,' she said hastily. 'The hagstone just showed me pictures of you. I shouldn't have read what you were writing, but I did. I saw what you said about not thinking I could heal Kestrel and about how much ...' She swallowed, her throat feeling tight as she looked at the floor. 'How much fun you had with Fran and Katie yesterday and –'

'Hang on! What diary? I haven't got a diary!' interrupted Chloe.

Erin looked up. 'You have. I saw you writing in it.'

'No,' said Chloe, shaking her head violently. 'You can't have. I really don't have a diary, Erin.'

Seeing the confusion in her eyes, Erin stared. A horrible thought dawned on her. 'Oh, Chloe,' she whispered. 'You don't think it was Marianne, do you? Using her magic to make me see visions?'

Chloe caught her breath. 'I bet it was. We know she can cast visions, make people see things. That's part of weather weaving, like when you cast an image of Tor into the skies. And Marianne's done it before. Remember, she sent a vision of Tor being ill-treated to Mistral, which is one of the reasons why he came through the gateway.'

Erin put her hands to her mouth. She couldn't believe she had been so dumb. 'I just didn't think about that. I wonder if they all came from her? Maybe she sent the one about the feather too, to get me in the house? But what about the vision about the hair?'

'That must have been the stones,' said Chloe. 'She'd hardly have sent you a vision to show you where your great-grandmother's hair was when she knows how powerful that could make you.' She stared at Erin. 'I can't believe she was making you see me writing stuff about you in a diary.'

Erin shook her head. 'I should have known you wouldn't think those things.'

'Of course I wouldn't,' said Chloe. 'As if I'd ever think Fran and Katie were loads of fun to hang around with. They drive me mad! I just didn't want to be mean by saying they couldn't ride Ziggy. But, you know, it was really cool when you got cross at Fran. I wanted to clap and cheer!'

They grinned at each other.

Chloe's voice became more serious. 'Marianne's been trying to make us argue, to split us up, you know.'

'Well, we're not going to let her do that,' Erin declared. 'We're in this together!'

'Yeah.' Chloe nodded fiercely. 'Together! Come on, let's go and tell Tor what's been happening.'

'And see if he knows how I can use Great-grandmother Margaret's hair to make my power stronger,' Erin added.

As they flew to the woods, Erin told
Chloe about Kestrel. Chloe was
delighted. 'That's brilliant!' she said,
turning a somersault. 'Oh, Erin!
We'll be able to ride whenever we
want, go out on hacks, go to shows.
Everything!'

'But we'll still help Jackie with the
other ponies,' Erin said.

'Of course,' grinned Chloe. 'The more
ponies, the better!'

Erin smiled happily; it was the best feeling ever having Chloe back as her best friend. They swooped down through the trees. Tor and Mistral were waiting for them.

'Loads has been happening!' Erin gasped.

She and Chloe told Tor and Mistral what had been going on. 'You were very lucky to escape,' said Tor in alarm. 'And I'm sure you are right, that some of the visions did come from the stones themselves. Marianne would not have known about Margaret's hair or she would have used it herself.'

'What does Erin have to do with the hair, Father?' asked Mistral.

'It is simple.' Tor looked at Erin. 'All you have to do is to wind one of your great-grandmother's hairs on to a hagstone and then whenever you use that hagstone to do magic, your great-grandmother's powers will be added to yours.'

'You'll be like ultra-powerful when you use that stone!' exclaimed Chloe.

Erin took a deep breath. She wasn't sure she wanted to be ultra-powerful. But if it meant she could cast visions again and maybe clear the skies so Tor could go through the gateway then she would do it. It didn't look as if Marianne was going to come back of her own accord.

She took one of her great-grandmother's grey hairs out of the envelope and felt in her pocket for a hagstone. She had a seeing stone with her, a healing stone and a warding stone that could be used to protect her against harm. It hadn't done much good in Marianne's study, but she wasn't very good at warding magic yet. She wound the hair through the seeing stone several times and tied the ends.

'There,' she said, holding it up.

'This might seem simple,' Tor told her. 'The rest will not. We must now bring Marianne back from the sky, get the hagstone from her and destroy her dark gateway.'

'How are we going to bring Marianne back, Father?' Mistral asked, pawing eagerly at the soft ground.

'We will go to the entrance of the hidden gateway down by the sea. When we are there, Erin and I will try to clear the clouds for long enough for the gateway to appear in the moonlight. You and I will go through the gateway and together we will chase Marianne down from the sky. It is our land, our kingdom. She has no right to be there.' Tor's eyes flashed with pride and he reared up on his hind legs. Erin suddenly realized he was relishing the thought of fighting the dark spirit who had been controlling and damaging his herd. He plunged forward, swirling into his cloud form. 'Come! There is no time to waste!'

With a wild, delighted whinny, Mistral galloped beside him.

Erin and Chloe flew through the trees as the horses galloped beneath them, their cloud bodies moving like the wind. Erin's heart was beating fast. Everything was suddenly happening! She gripped the hagstone in her hand. Might they really stop Marianne that very night?

When they reached the edge of the woods, Tor and Mistral soared into the sky and, together with the girls, they swooped over the cliff top and down to the beach. Usually the jagged rocks were covered with deep water, but now at low tide there were just glittering rock pools. The entrance to the hidden gateway was almost completely blocked by a rockfall.

'We will do the magic to clear the clouds here,' Tor said to Erin. 'You must be ready to use your great-grandmother's powers to face Marianne when she returns and get the hagstone from her.' He touched her shoulder. 'Do not worry. I will be following her. You will not be on your own.'

'She won't be on her own anyway. I'll
be here,' said Chloe fiercely, moving to
stand alongside Erin.

Erin picked up a sharp shard of stone
from one of the rock pools and, pressing
hard, scratched a circle on one of the
largest, flattest rocks. Then she took the
hagstone with her great-grandmother's
hair out of her pocket and began.

The second she stared at the hole in
the stone with her great-grandmother's
hair tied through it, the darkness
expanded. She gasped as magic surged

through her. Not the tingling that she usually felt, but rushing, racing, sweeping through her like a swift-flowing river, as the power of her great-grandmother joined with her own power. Erin had never felt anything like it. Every inch of her skin seemed to crackle with magic. She felt strong and powerful, able to do anything.

'Sky horses, come!' she commanded.

This time they didn't appear slowly. They were suddenly there in the circle, manes and tails blowing, ears flickering. Many looked sick. Marianne had been in the cloud world for too long. Foals were lying down, mares nuzzling them with dull eyes. But as Tor appeared they raised their heads, nudged the foals, made them get up. The herd gathered round him, whickering in relief. He whinnied to them all. They followed him obediently, clearing the circle and clearing the clouds from the moon overhead.

At the edge of the circle Erin saw a dark cloud forming. Marianne! There was no time to waste!

'Tor! Come back! Sky horses, be gone!'

The sky horses vanished.

Erin scrambled to her feet as Tor swirled to his normal size.

'Mistral! We must go through the gateway before Marianne brings the clouds back!' He gave the girls a searching look. 'Be ready for when we return! Who knows what will happen then . . .' And he leapt away, dissolving into a mist that flowed past the rockfall into the cave. Mistral followed him. There was a faint whinny and they were gone. The silence was broken only by the sound of the sea creeping back in towards the cliffs and the cry of a seagull overhead.

Erin looked at Chloe.

'Now what?' Chloe said.

'We wait, I guess,' replied Erin. She went over to the cave and looked at the gap between the rockfall and the wall. It was just big enough for her to squeeze through. She knew the cave behind it led to a tunnel, which led to another underground cave where the gateway was. Tor and Mistral would have gone through it by now. She wondered what was happening.

'You looked different when you did the magic just then,' said Chloe, joining her.

'I felt different,' admitted Erin. 'Everything happened so much more quickly than normal. It was weird. There was all this power flowing through me. I felt like I was almost going to explode with it.'

Chloe crossed her arms, pretending to be annoyed. 'It's not fair. You have all the fun!'

Erin knew Chloe was joking, trying to help ease her tension as they waited anxiously. 'Yeah, yeah,' she said. 'I know you wish you were me. You're just jealous! You *so* wish you could fight Marianne later!'

There was a cold laugh behind them. 'Not later, Erin. *Now!*'

They both swung round.

Marianne was standing on the rocks, just a few metres away from them, her silvery-blue dress swirling around her, a spiteful smile on her face.

Eleven

Marianne raised her hands and pointed at Erin. 'Bind her!' she hissed.

Chloe leapt out of the way, but Erin didn't move fast enough.

Marianne's magic hit her, knocking her off her feet and slamming her into the cliff face. She was pinned there, as if an invisible giant hand was holding her against the rocks. It was a powerful binding spell. Erin knew the only way to break free was to distract the attention of the dark spirit.

'Hello, Erin,' Marianne said, triumph glittering in her eyes.

Chloe started to raise her hand.

'Don't even think about it!' snarled Marianne, her eyes flicking in Chloe's direction. She tightened the fingers of the hand that was pointing at Erin. Erin felt herself being pushed harder against the rock and she cried out.

Chloe quickly lowered her hand.

'In any case, why bother?' said Marianne. 'I know you hate her for having so much power and being able to do more magic than you can. And now she has more magic than ever at her disposal.' Marianne's eyes bored into Chloe. 'I understand you, girl. In your heart, you do not want to save her.'

Erin saw Chloe start to open her

mouth to argue. Then suddenly she seemed to change her mind. 'You're right,' Chloe said softly.

Erin stared, wondering for a moment if Marianne had placed her under some sort of spell. But Chloe's eyes flicked towards her and just for the briefest second Erin saw a look that said *trust me*. Chloe started backing away. 'I'm sorry, Erin. I can't help you this time.'

Erin picked up the faintest tremor in Chloe's voice, but Marianne didn't seem to notice. A smile curved at the dark spirit's mouth as if she was pleased with herself. 'Go then,' she snapped. 'I have no interest in you.' Chloe turned and flew away.

Although Erin was sure Chloe had some plan, it was horrible to be left alone with Marianne. The dark spirit advanced

on her. Erin felt as if her blood had
turned to icy water.

'So, you have my sister's power now,'
mused Marianne. 'Everyone said that she
was going to be the most powerful
weather weaver who ever lived. No one
ever gave a thought to me. But that was
only because I was younger. I had as
much power as my sister did, just no one
ever knew.' The dark spirit's eyes
gleamed. 'My sister never captured a sky
stallion. She never went into the cloud
world. She never controlled the weather
as I have.'

'That's because she knew it was
wrong!' Erin burst out, unable to stop
herself. 'She knew you shouldn't do it!
She knew it would make the horses'
magic go. She –'

'Be silent!' screamed Marianne.

Erin recoiled against the rock.

There was a silence then, and when Marianne spoke it was in a hiss, grinding out the words. 'It wasn't because she didn't want to do it. It was because she *couldn't* do it. Her power was less than mine. And now I have the chance to

prove it. You have Margaret's hair, but I am in control now and once you are gone no one will stop me from ruling the cloud kingdom. I will defeat the stallion and his son and then the sky horses will do as I demand – always.' She pulled a hagstone out of her pocket. It had two strands of hair wrapped round it. 'This is what you want, isn't it, Erin? The stone that holds my dark gateway. You want to destroy it. Well, here.' She held it out. 'Take it,' she taunted. But Erin couldn't move. She couldn't do anything to break Marianne's hold over her.

'Oh dear,' Marianne chuckled. 'You are helpless even with Margaret's power. This is just too easy.'

'What are you going to do to me?' Erin's throat was dry.

'Destroy you, my dear,' Marianne said. 'And then you will never get in my way again.' Her eyes gleamed madly. She clicked her fingers and, behind her, Erin saw the water of the sea begin to move. It swirled faster and faster in a circle. To her horror she saw it start to rise up in a funnel shape. It looked as though it was a tornado, but made of water. It grew bigger and bigger until it was twice the size of a person. It began to spin towards them over the rocks, swirling up seaweed, stones and driftwood, making a horrible grinding, rushing noise as it approached.

Terror slammed through Erin. It was coming straight for her. The noise filled her ears as the funnel of water got closer and closer. 'So much power and yet you can't stop me!' shouted Marianne above the sound of the whirling water.

'She can't, but maybe I can!' Chloe's voice yelled from up above. 'Fire be with me!'

Two arrows of glowing fire shot down from the sky. Erin couldn't see where Chloe was because she was camouflaged, but her aim was good. The first arrow hit Marianne on her back, the second on her shoulder. As they made contact, they exploded into harmless showers of sparks. Erin realized Marianne must have a warding stone protecting her. But even though the arrows didn't hurt the dark spirit, they distracted her. She swung round in shock.

Erin seized her chance to escape. Drawing on all the power that was inside her, she moved her hand just enough to grab the hagstone in her pocket. As her fingers closed on it, her great-grandmother's power exploded through her too. She shot into the air, the binding spell loosening instantly. 'No!' Marianne shrieked.

'Marianne! The whirlpool!' yelled Erin as the giant water tornado spun towards the rock the dark spirit was standing on, pulling up everything that it met. But Marianne's attention was too focused on Erin. Opening her mouth, she screamed in rage: 'Bind –'

But before the dark spirit could finish, the vortex was upon her. It engulfed her, sweeping her up inside its watery funnel. For a moment Erin saw Marianne's shocked face, saw her stagger back, her arms flailing as she dropped the hagstone in her hand. She made a wild grab for it, but the swirling water swallowed her up. She disappeared with a loud shriek. Erin saw a flash of her silvery-blue dress blur past as the water spun faster and faster, clattering, rushing, swirling, and then all of a sudden the water tornado completely vanished.

There was silence. Just an empty space where the whirlpool had been.

Chloe appeared in the sky, her face shocked. 'Where's it gone? Where's Marianne?'

Erin stared. 'I don't know.' She flew down and landed on the rocks. There was no sign of the whirlpool or Marianne at all. She shuddered. Marianne had been planning to use the whirlpool to destroy her. It must have done the same to the dark spirit herself. She turned to Chloe wordlessly.

Chloe flew over and hugged her hard.

'You rescued me,' said Erin. 'And with arrows of fire!'

Chloe smiled shakily. 'I don't know if it's what the prophecy meant, but it just seemed the right thing to do. Oh, Erin, it was so lucky Marianne let me go when she bound you otherwise I couldn't have distracted her like that. I can't believe she really thought I'd go off and leave you!'

'She believed it because that's what she would have done,' Erin said slowly. 'She was so twisted up by jealousy. I think that was what brought her back from the sky tonight. She wanted to prove she had more power than Margaret by destroying me while Tor was out of the way, before going back to fight him. I'm so glad you came back.'

Chloe took Erin's hand. For a moment everything that had happened swirled between them like a raging wind. It was too big for words.

'Erin!' They heard a whinny and looked round. Tor and Mistral were sweeping out of the cave entrance as mist. They formed into horses on the rocks. 'Where's Marianne?' Tor demanded, looking about him.

'She's gone,' whispered Erin.

Erin and Chloe explained everything that had happened while Tor and Mistral had been in the cloud kingdom trying to track Marianne down. Tor did not know where the whirlpool had gone, but he felt it unlikely that the dark spirit would have survived.

'The whirlpool was made from her magic,' he said. 'I think it probably vanished as its creator perished. And if Marianne has perished, then the dark gateway will have perished too – for it sprang from her powers as well as yours. If it has been destroyed, your own powers will have returned, Erin.'

Erin took out the hagstone from her pocket and untied her great-grandmother's hair. Chloe marked out a new circle for her. Erin looked at the hole in the stone. Her heart beat fast. Would her magic work with just her power alone?

'Sky horses, come,' she said.

Clouds started to swell at the edge of

the circle. They formed into horse shapes.
Some were standing, but many were
lying down. They looked sad and ill.

'My power's back!' breathed Erin. 'But
what about your herd?'

Tor stepped forward. 'You can help
them with your healing magic.'

Erin frowned. 'How? I can't use it from
down here, can I?'

'No, but you can use it in the clouds.'

Erin stared at him. 'You want me to come to the clouds? But won't that make the horses more sick?'

'It will only be a brief visit and I believe your presence with a healing stone will do far more good than harm. My herd need you, Erin.'

Erin glanced at Chloe. She loved the thought of going to the cloud world, but how would Chloe feel?

Chloe forced a smile. 'It's OK. You go. I know I can't come. It won't be good for the horses.'

'I'll stay with you, Chloe,' said Mistral. And Chloe hugged him.

Erin turned to Tor. 'How do I get there?'

He stamped a front hoof. 'Through the

hidden gateway we discovered by the aspen tree.'

Leaving Chloe and Mistral on the rocks, Erin squeezed into the cave. Tor dissolved and flowed in beside her. It was too small a space for him to turn into his horse shape, but she could feel his presence like a cool wind swirling around her as she flew down the dark tunnel to the second cave.

This cave was bigger than the first and Tor turned back into his solid earthly horse shape. On the floor there was a perfect circle of moonlight. *The hidden gateway*, Erin thought.

'Get on my back,' Tor told her softly.

A thrill ran through Erin. Never in her wildest dreams had she ever imagined riding Tor. She took hold of his long mane and vaulted on. His back felt warm and strong, his arched neck rose up in front of her, his long mane covering her legs.

Tor whickered and stepped into the circle of light on the floor. Suddenly they were swirling round and round in a golden haze. For a moment the only solid thing seemed to be Tor's body. Erin flung herself forward on his neck, holding on tight, as night and day, ice and sunlight – the very fabric of the world – seemed to blur and spin around her.

CHAPTER

Twelve

They landed. Erin blinked and sat up on
Tor's back. They were standing in a cloud
meadow. There were jagged mountains
and forests in the distance, valleys and
streams. But Erin hardly noticed the
landscape. She was staring at the sky
horses in front of her.

She had seen them many times before
through the stones, but in real life they
were ten times more beautiful. They
reminded her of Kestrel with their large

dark eyes and dished faces, delicate legs and pointed ears. There were foals, mares, young stallions, all standing still. Tor walked forward with Erin on his back. 'This is my kingdom,' he told her.

'Oh wow!' Erin gasped. 'And there's Snowdance!'

The beautiful mare came trotting forward, her hooves seeming to dance across the ground. She touched noses with Tor. 'This is Erin,' Tor said.

Snowdance whinnied in greeting. Erin slid off Tor's back. The ground was white and springy beneath her feet. She looked at the stallion. She knew she should be as quick as she could. 'Shall I start?' she asked, feeling almost shy.

'Yes.'

Erin took the healing stone out of her

pocket and walked towards the first group, four mares and foals who were all lying down, their muzzles resting on the ground. Murmuring soothingly, just as she had done to Kestrel when he was injured, she moved among them, touching the stone to each of them, one at a time, until she felt it turn from cold to warm. After each horse, she paused to recharge it, holding it in her hands, concentrating hard, thinking healing thoughts. The difference it made to the horses was noticeable. As she stepped back from each one, they raised their heads, looked around, pricked their ears and got to their feet.

Other horses started to crowd round her. Soon she was lost in a sea of grey bodies and swirling manes. She stroked and patted, touched the stone to horse after horse. They tossed their heads as the stone's magic worked.

Erin turned to Tor at last. 'That's it.' She looked about. The cloud land was now a very different place than when she had arrived. The horses were grazing, trotting, the foals playing, the mares nuzzling each other and scratching each other's necks. Their eyes were bright and calm and happy.

Tor walked over to her. 'Thank you,' Tor said softly. His eyes met hers and Erin instinctively knew it was time to go. She got on to his back and wrapped her hands in his mane. He cantered forward, his neck arched, his ears pricked. Erin could see the magical gateway in front of them. It looked like a giant hagstone made out of clouds. For a moment the cloud world swept by and then she felt Tor gather himself up and leap into the air. Clutching his mane, they soared through the gateway and then they were gently spiralling down and down in a golden haze until they landed in a clatter of hooves. Erin blinked in the darkness of the cave as Tor stopped.

'We're back,' she whispered, realizing they were inside the cave.

'Yes,' said Tor. 'And it is time to say goodbye.'

Erin slipped off his back and looked at him. The moonlight was still flooding through the hole in the cave roof. She could see the sadness shining in his eyes.

'But not goodbye forever, Tor. We can keep this gateway open. Only Chloe and I know about it now Marianne's gone. I know we mustn't come to the cloud world, but you and Mistral could come here and see us sometimes.' The words tumbled desperately out of her even though she knew in her heart what Tor was going to say.

'No, Erin. The gateway must be

sealed. The two worlds should not mix.'

'But we won't come through. You can come to us. It'll be all right,' said Erin, her voice rising. She couldn't bear to say goodbye to Tor forever.

'It won't,' said Tor gently. 'Who knows who else Marianne told about this gateway. She lived for many, many years. We cannot take the risk that someone else will use it. You must seal it and keep it sealed, just as your mother did before you.'

Erin looked at him. He really meant it – she was going to have to close the gateway. 'But . . . but I can't say goodbye to you!' she burst out desperately.

'You must. You have Chloe, your family.' Tor stepped forward. 'We'll still be able to talk through the hagstones. Even if we cannot see each other in this way, we will still be part of each other's lives. I will watch you down here, and you can watch me in the skies.'

'But I don't want to just watch you! I want to see you,' Erin whispered, tears starting to prickle in her eyes. After all they had been through, to lose him, to never see him again . . .

A sob burst from her.

Tor touched her face, but didn't speak, and then she really knew that she was going to have to say goodbye. She flung her arms round his neck and, burying her head in his long mane, started to cry.

Tor nuzzled her shoulder tenderly until her sobs slowed down. She took a

deep, trembling breath and rubbed away
the damp on her face with the backs of
her hands.

'We should go, Erin,' he said softly.
'Chloe and Mistral will be wondering
where we are. It is not quite goodbye yet.'
He swirled into mist. Moving slowly, her
thoughts in turmoil, Erin walked along
the tunnel, sensing him beside her.

'You're back!' said Chloe in relief as
Erin squeezed out past the rockfall. 'Is
everything OK?' she asked, seeing Erin's
face.

Erin didn't know what to say. She felt
numb, like her heart had been frozen.

Tor formed out of the mist beside her.
'The sky horses are healed, Chloe. The
skies are calm. Without you two, this
could never have happened.'

'I'm just glad everything's OK now.' Chloe looked uncertainly at Erin. 'It *is* OK, isn't it?'

Erin forced the words past the lump in her throat. 'We . . . we can't keep the gateway open,' she said, not able to meet Chloe's eyes.

'We have to say goodbye, Chloe,' Tor added quietly. 'It is the only way.'

Mistral walked over and nuzzled them and Erin realized Tor must have already told him. 'I'll never forget you,' the foal said to them both.

'But I don't want you to go!' Chloe burst out, tears springing to her eyes too as she hugged him fiercely.

Tor walked over to her. 'We have to.'

Erin put a hand on his neck, her gaze running over his head, his body. She

didn't want to stop looking at the two
sky horses, didn't want to imagine a time
when she couldn't see them any more.

'Thank you for everything,' said Tor,
nuzzling Chloe.

Chloe stroked him. 'G-goodbye, Tor.'

Tor stepped towards Erin and put his
muzzle to her forehead. 'When you look
up, I'll be there,' he said softly. 'Always.'

Fresh tears filled her eyes. She tried to

hold them back, but they spilt silently down her cheeks.

Tor turned to Mistral. 'Come!'

The two horses reared up. For a moment they were silhouetted against the starry sky. Then they swirled into mist and swept past the rockfall in a glittering haze for the last time.

Come back! Erin cried in her mind.

But the sky horses had gone.

'So that's really goodbye?' whispered Chloe as if she couldn't quite believe it.

Erin stared at the cave, her heart aching. 'Yes.'

Trying to block out her unhappiness, she knelt down and opened her bag. 'Let's seal the gateway,' she said numbly. Now Tor had gone, she just wanted to do what she had to do and leave. She took out the diary, the silver bowl, the crystal bottle, the pot of earth, the candle and the feather.

She led the way into the cave and through to the gateway. Then, laying out the things she needed, she followed her mum's instructions in the diary, trying not to think about Tor or Mistral. Trying not to think about anything. She finished by holding the hagstone in the centre of the circle of moonlight.

'Be sealed,' she whispered. The silver circle shivered and then was still.

'That's it,' Erin said. 'It's done.' She stared at the gateway for a moment. 'I'm . . . I'm going to miss them.'

'Me too.' Chloe looked at her in the moonlight. 'But I know you'll miss Tor more.' She took a deep breath. 'At least you can still talk to him with your weather weaving, Erin. He's right, it isn't goodbye forever. And although I know it's going to be horrible not seeing him and Mistral, at least Marianne's gone. There won't be any more great storms now and there are lots of fun things we can still do – stardust stuff in the evenings and riding Kestrel and Ziggy in the day.' She took Erin's hands and squeezed them. 'It will be OK.'

Erin slowly smiled at her. 'Yes,' she said, believing her as always. 'It will.' And she knew it was true.

Afterwards . . .

Dear Mum,

I know I haven't written much the last two weeks, but it's been so busy! I thought everything would be quiet after Tor and Mistral had gone, but then Xanthe, Allegra's mum, invited me and Chloe to stay with her and Allegra for three nights. I met all of Allegra's friends and Xanthe showed us how to start using different stardust magic. Her ankle's getting better now. We learnt loads. Xanthe told us we have higher powers. I'm not very good at using mine yet, but Chloe

can make invisible shields. She's really good at
that! When we got back we found out that
there's a pony club show on this weekend so
we've been practising for that too. Kestrel's
brilliant at jumping! And Ziggy's the fastest
at all the gymkhana games. Anyway, I'd better
go now because Chloe and I are going to the
stables early and then Chloe's coming back
here for a sleepover tonight. Tomorrow we're
going to bath the ponies for the show. I can't
wait to tell you about how it goes. More soon,
I promise!

Erin and Chloe rode on to the beach. It
was early in the morning and the sands
were empty apart from a few dog-walkers.
The sun was just rising in the sky, its rays
glittering on the water. The tide was

going out. The sand was damp and firm beneath the ponies' hooves.

Erin sighed happily. The whole summer was stretching out ahead. Kestrel and Ziggy tossed their heads, their bits jangling. They wanted to gallop.

Chloe looked challengingly at Erin. 'Race you to the breakers!'

Erin didn't even bother to say yes. 'Ready, steady, go!' she shouted, throwing herself forward on Kestrel's neck.

The two ponies raced along the beach, their hooves pounding on the sand.

Erin glanced upwards. Overhead, a white cloud in the shape of a stallion was flowing across the sky.

When you look up, I'll be there, Tor's voice echoed in her head.

She smiled. He was there, just as he
had said.

For always.